The Stratford Devil

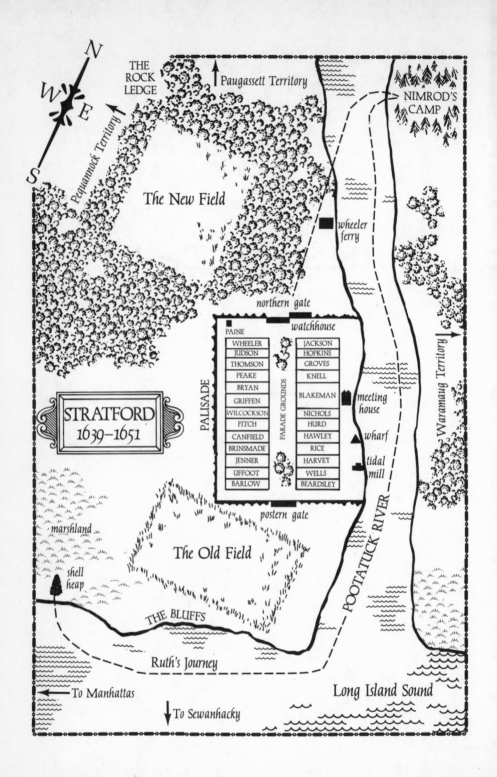

N
W · E
S

THE ROCK LEDGE

Paugassett Territory

Pequannock Territory

Waramaug Territory

The New Field

NIMROD'S CAMP

wheeler ferry

northern gate

watchhouse

PAINE

PALISADE

PARADE GROUNDS

WHEELER
JUDSON
THOMSON
PEAKE
BRYAN
GRIFFEN
WILCOCKSON
FITCH
CANFIELD
BRINSMADE
JENNER
UFFOOT
BARLOW

JACKSON
HOPKINS
GROVES
KNELL
BLAKEMAN
NICHOLS
HURD
HAWLEY
RICE
HARVEY
WELLS
BEARDSLEY

meeting house

wharf

tidal mill

STRATFORD 1639–1651

marshland

shell heap

The Old Field

postern gate

POOTATUCK RIVER

THE BLUFFS

Ruth's Journey

To Manhattas

To Sewanhacky

Long Island Sound

THE STRATFORD DEVIL

Claude Clayton Smith

WALKER AND COMPANY
NEW YORK

Walker's American History Series for Young People
Series Editor, Frances Nankin

The author wishes to thank Donald W. Fowler, past president
of the Stratford Historical Society, for providing access
to the society's museum, and for recommending William H.
Wilcoxson's *History of Stratford, Connecticut 1639-1969*.

First published in the United States of America in 1984
by the Walker Publishing Company, Inc.

Published simultaneously in Canada by John Wiley & Sons
Canada, Limited, Rexdale, Ontario.

Library of Congress Cataloging in Publication Data

Smith, Claude Clayton, 1944-
The Stratford Devil.

(Walker's American history series for young people)
Summary: A young girl named Ruth is a witness to events leading to the hanging of
Goody Bassett for witchcraft in the town of Stratford, Connecticut, in the spring of
1651.
1. Stratford (Conn.)—History—Juvenile fiction.
2. Connecticut—History—Colonial period, ca. 1600-1775—Juvenile fiction.
[1.Witchcraft—Fiction. 2. Connecticut—History—Colonial period, ca. 1600-
1775—Fiction]
I. Title. II. Series.
PZ7.S64463St 1984 [Fic] 84-19684
ISBN 0-8027-6544-0

Printed in the United States of America

10 9 8 7 6 5 4 3 2 1

Book Design by Teresa Carboni

To Elaine

Contents

Author's Note

In the spring of 1651, a woman known as Goody Bassett was hanged for witchcraft in the town of Stratford, Connecticut. It was the second such execution in Connecticut, nearly half a century before the notorious witch trials in Salem, Massachusetts. Known facts in the case are few. The characters of Ruth, Widow Paine, Jonas Paine, Pervis, and Charles Bassett are based on scant historical evidence and remain largely fictional. Other characters, as well as the setting and threats of Indians and wolves, are based on detailed accounts of the early history of Stratford, which I adapt to my tale.

PART I

Stratford, 1640

1.

The Terns

"*SHOULD'ST?*"

As if to answer her own question, Ruth gazed across the Sound to the long island the Red Man called Sewenhacky. Today, in the sparkling bright air of midsummer, it was plainly visible, a low dark stretch of land along the southern horizon. Soft clouds stood banked above it, as white as wool.

The first time Ruth had seen the island, entering the mouth of the Pootatuck River with Reverend Blakeman's tiny band of settlers, she had thought it was England. What was all the fuss? she had wondered. How could it take two months to sail from the Old World? Eight stormy weeks from here to there? Impossible.

Big Moses Wheeler had laughed heartily. "If that be England, child, then this be France, and we have sailed in the wrong direction!"

Others laughed, too—Sergeant Nichols, Thomas Hawley, Nicolas Knell—and the Puritan children pointed their fingers and jeered. But it was an honest mistake. Ruth had not sailed with them to the New World in the *Planter* or the *Hopewell*. She had been born in Massachusetts Bay, raised by the Widow Paine at the trading post now called Windsor, one of the earliest settlements in the Connecticut Colony.

"*Should'st?*"

Again Ruth considered her whim, and her tongue curled to the tip of her long, straight nose. It was a habit she had while daydreaming, one for which Goodman Peake, the sexton and bell-ringer, frequently switched her during Sabbath services, whispering loud enough for all to hear, "Pay attention, child, lest the Devil take thee!"

But on *this* Sabbath morning she was free of that.

High above the grassy bluff on which she stood, a sleek tern wheeled and dove. *Kee-urr! Kee-urr!* Its harsh cries seemed an invitation. *Come on! Come on!*

Running to the edge, Ruth tucked her frock between her knees and slid down the steep, bumpy slope. At the bottom, she brushed herself off and ran across the long line of debris left by the change of tide—clumps of seaweed, sticks of driftwood, broken shells—straight to the water's edge.

Kee-urr! Kee-urr!

The gray tern slapped the Sound and sailed away on an off-shore breeze, a small fish twisting in its red-orange bill. Others followed in delirious, buoyant flight, their black-tipped wings and forked tails cutting across the solid blue sky. *Kee-urr! Kee-urr! Come on!*

"I should!" Ruth concluded without delay.

Drawing her drab smock over her head, she tossed it aside and, naked, touched a toe to the chilly, rippling water. Her gangling twelve-year-old body trembled, breasts erect, as small and hard as crabapples.

Reaching back, elbows like wings, she untied the leather cord at the nape of her neck, and her frizzy red hair shook free. She raised her face to the sun, letting the dry heat bathe the blemishes that had recently appeared. Perhaps the salt water would wash them away. Was not the sea a powerful healer?

She plunged on in. The water shocked her body, icy but exhilarating. Her hair clung to her face, and she wiped it aside. "Oh where are ye, heathen?" she laughed. "Where are ye, wild beasts?"

Palms down, she splashed the water and dove again, her body

loose and easy beneath the surface, free of the cramped awkwardness that had plagued her in recent days.

No, she hadn't lied to Widow Paine. She *had* felt ill first thing in the morning, strangely uncomfortable. Her body was in some sort of rebellion, like a snake shedding its skin. Her arms and legs didn't fit her joints. She needed a new set of bones.

Surfacing once more, Ruth shivered, the shifting breeze prickling her skin. Turning, she waded ashore, grabbed her smock, and hurried to the base of the bluffs.

"Skinny as a swamp reed, Master John Blakeman? And coarse sedge grass for hair? Well, sir, how do ye find me now?" She laughed and curled her tongue to her nose, wondering what the Reverend's eldest son would think when he saw her place empty, on the split-log bench at the rear of the Meeting House. She laughed again, picturing Goodman Hawley turning the hourglass for the second time.

Wrestling her smock over her head and bony shoulders, she scrambled up the bluff to look back along the way she had come.

Far to the east, the sweet water of the Pootatuck River widened into a bay where it met the Sound. Upstream lay the settlement, in a marshy cove the Indians called *cupheag*, or "place of shelter." The settlers had renamed it Sandy Hollow.

The palisade, a long line of wide, slablike stakes set close together in the earth, bounded the home-lots on three sides; the river protected its east flank. The fortification stood ten feet high. It had been among the first concerns of the settlers, erected even as they built their crude log dwellings. In the long year since its completion, Ruth had not once been outside it until now.

West of the palisade lay the common pastures to which the cattle and sheep were led daily to graze. To the south was the Old Field, where the men labored during the week under the safety of sentinels. Now, in the full bloom of summer, the field stood tall with waving tassels of leafy corn. Through the center of the Old Field ran the narrow path along which Ruth had escaped barefoot to reach the bluffs.

In the opposite direction, far to the west, the bluffs diminished and dwindled to a point. Brackish tidal ponds replaced them, continuing along the irregular coastline in a hundred tiny inlets fringed with cattails.

"Let us embrace the shining bosom of the land!" Reverend Adam Blakeman had said so often, causing Goodman Peake to break out his switch against the titters among the children in the back rows.

Ruth wondered if her own bosoms would ever grow, to become as broad and heavy as Widow Paine's. Of late they had been tender and sore.

About to turn for home, she stared intently up the shore to where the line of bluffs receded, a mile or more away. Something—a brilliant gleaming—had caught her eye.

At first it appeared to be nothing more than the sun reflecting on the water's shiny surface, but studying it further, Ruth perceived that it was on the beach itself, in a stretch of dazzling white sand.

Bigger than a bonfire yet without leaping flames, the flashing continued, a bright beacon even in broadest daylight.

The terns swept in from the water and glided on ahead, darting and diving until they became too thin to see. Their screaming died away behind them: *Kee-urr! Kee-urr!* Come on!

Ruth followed through the tall grass, the spinelike clumps cutting her feet, eyes fixed on the distant gleaming.

Closer still, the source of light grew in size, glittering like a haystack of gems and jewels. Ruth began to run, ignoring the cramp that soon nailed her in the side.

The terns, it seemed, were already there, joined by a flock of gulls in the corner of the sky.

At a hundred yards, the light was blinding. The bluffs ended. Ruth slowed to a walk. Short of breath, she shaded her eyes with both hands and hiked across a shallow dune to reach the beach.

The hot sand, whiter here than along the bluffs, seared her feet, but she ignored it as she did the pain in her side.

A tremendous mound sat high up on the beach, beyond the reach of the cresting tides. It was four times her height and wider than a barn door. Intense heat radiated from it, rippling the air.

Only when she stood beside it, squinting intensely, did Ruth recognize the shells—oyster shells, clam shells, mussels and crabs—a million shells in a heap as solid as pearl.

Falling to her knees, she plucked a handful from the pile. The sun had bleached them like bones and baked them to a fragile brittleness. Even the mussels, those miniature black canoes that dotted the beach, had been broiled to a light gray, spicing the huge stack like salt and pepper.

The mound was odorless, the steady salt breezes having done their work. Not a shred of meat remained. The shells were picked clean, as fresh as the morning itself.

Ruth tossed an oyster shell from hand to hand—light, thin, hot to the touch, and dry as dust. Fine grooves swept outward from a central point on the surface in continuous, intricate swirls. Running her fingernail through them, Ruth noticed that many of the shells were broken, as if they had been dashed into the pile.

Kee-urr! Kee-urr! Circling above, the terns seemed to claim responsibility for the collosal heap.

Ruth looked into the sky. The site was too magnificent to be the handiwork of gulls or terns. The shells must have been accumulated over hundreds of years. But how? *By whom?*

She would ask Nicolas Knell about them, as soon as she could catch him alone. Goodman Knell was old and wise and knew everything, even if—and the thought caused Ruth to glance about her—it might concern itself with the Red Man.

The Red Man wore shell necklaces, but with shells much

smaller than these. She had seen them hanging from the necks of the warriors captured in the Great Pequot War, in the decisive battles that opened the fertile Connecticut valleys to the settlers. The Red Man had killed her Papa, Jonas Paine. Shortly thereafter, Widow Paine had taken her from Windsor to Wethersfield, to join Reverend Blakeman's little group on its way to Sandy Hollow.

The memory was disturbing. Ruth squatted in the short shadow at the base of the mound. The rippling heat was making her dizzy.

In the band of shade the sand was noticeably cooler, as white and fine as the sand in Reverend Blakeman's hourglass, sand that at this very moment, Ruth knew, was marking the minutes of the Sabbath service.

She poured it back and forth, letting it slip through her fingers, then dusted her hands on her smock and plucked away a few more shells. Squatting above them, feet apart, she used the shells to spell out her name, the only word she knew how to write.

Clam, oyster, mussel; clam, oyster, mussel. She alternated the shells, pleased with her craft. Finished, she curled her tongue to the tip of her nose. R-U-T-H.

What would the terns make of her message? What would the Red Man say?

The sun blistered above the heap, heating her scalp, drying her wet hair. The salt air seemed excited, annoyed. The terns suddenly fled, their shadows flitting like bats across the sand, but the gulls remained, circling more widely.

Ruth stood quickly, dwarfed by the mysterious mound. She felt ill, nauseous, weak from running. Stiff cramps wracked her abdomen. She wished she were at the Meeting House, safe within the palisade. She was intruding. Why had she come all this way?

She squatted again, trembling. Beneath her in the sand was a bright red dewdrop, a ruby she hadn't noticed before. As she touched it, the sand instantly absorbed it, leaving only a dull brown stain on her fingertip.

To the left of the first a second appeared. Then another, as red as last night's sunset. She touched them in turn and the sand took them like a sponge.

The rebellion was upon her again. The gulls ignored her. She sank to her knees, quivering, hugging herself as hard as she could.

2.

The Scent

THE breeze shifted innocently, stiff and steady from the east.
The surface of the river rippled. The Sound washed the coast
with small waves. To the west, at the edge of the green woods, a
timber wolf stirred, paws folded in its face, lethargic from a glut-
tonous meal.

Snapping erect, its short brown ears turned slowly. The
woods were silent.

The carcass of a deer, thick with flies, lay in the sun a few
yards away. Crows waited in the topmost branches of a nearby
oak.

The scent came again.

Raising its brown muzzle, the wolf tasted the wind, separating
its odors, ignoring the familiar doe carcass, the mice in the field,
a rabbit somewhere along the brook, its own urine on a clump
of sawgrass, marking a boundary where the woods met the
shore.

None of these was the cause of its waking.

Burying its face in its paws again, the wolf flipped to its side,
rolled, and stood up. It was a large and powerful male with a
broad head, strong limbs, and a deep, narrow chest. Its sturdy
shoulders stood three feet high. Rough, black-tipped hairs ran
the ridge of its spine, and its thick rust-red coat was laden with
burrs and small seeds.

Arching its back, the wolf stretched, shaking its head vigorously from side to side. A mosquito buzzed its ear, and it snapped its jaws.

Damp smells came, then warm smells, infoₗmation on every current of air. One by one, the wolf interpreted the signals and dismissed them.

Missing today were the steamy odors of cattle, the pungent scent of sheep. But there was a new and special smell, spiced by the tangy salt air. It was strangely familiar and yet unrecognized. Rousing memories, it was the kind of smell that made the wolf hungry again, although he had gorged on the doe at dawn.

Sorting it from the others, he regarded it with suspicion and curiosity. The breeze dropped an instant, then quickened, the enticing odor dancing away. Then it came round again, and the wolf left the coolness of the shade. Small prey moved off quietly at the edge of the meadow, a grouse and a covey of quail.

Catching the new scent, the wolf veered to the right in the direction of the Sound, avoiding the den of a skunk and a possible encounter.

Downwind, the crows immediately descended on the doe.

The wolf broke into a trot on a trail it had used many times. The skunk smell gone, others continued on the wind, dominated by the bittersweet annoyance that had nudged him from sleep.

Twice he stopped to inspect the ridges of old tracks, some his own, still firm in the mud. Twice he stopped to examine the cache of an old kill, clean bones in the brush, now a scent-post. Then he continued, driven by the odor on the wind, increasing speed, head and tail erect. He ran effortlessly, every movement smooth and deliberate, his body floating above large feet and spindly legs.

High white clouds lined the horizon above the distant cattails. Beyond the marshes lay white sand dunes and the Sound. Gulls circled in the distance, as if on guard.

Halfway across the meadow the wolf stopped in mid-stride,

legs firmly braced, head in the air. The disturbing scent had resolved itself into two, one that was bitter, the source of its fear, and another that was sweet, still unknown.

Moving to the side, the wolf sniffed a scent post, a tall thicket it had wet on other occasions. Then it rolled in the grass and ran on.

At the far edge of the meadow it stopped again, wetting high on a rock to make a new scent-post. It was more apprehensive now, out of its own territory.

The strange odor grew stronger. The thick pads of large feet touched down lightly. Tall reeds gave way silently, parted by the thrusting muzzle. Nearing the rim of an inlet, the wolf leaped every few strides, trying to see above the swaying cat-tails.

Soon he could see the gulls without leaping, revolving slowly in a wide, flat circle. *Kow-kow-kow.* Their calls diminished as he approached.

Then the odor of shells struck his nostrils on the same drift of wind as the peculiar scent. Off to the left a snapping turtle, large and green, slipped from a grassy pad and submerged itself up to its neck in a brackish pool, blinking its opaque eyes.

The wolf ignored it.

He paused to drink where fresh water bubbled up through a black mud spring. Unlike the brook in the woods, the water was warm, but it soothed his red tongue and thick throat.

Gradually the reeds lessened in height, growing thinner into waving dune oats, and the wolf emerged, wet to the flanks.

Now across the crest of a dune came a brilliant gleaming. The glare stabbed the wolf's eyes, as wild as fire. Acrid heat stung his nostrils.

He crossed the dune, the pads of his feet impervious to the burning sand. Keeping downwind, he approached the source of the scent.

The girl lay on her side in a shadow as broad and wide as the shell mound above her. She was motionless, eyes shut, head in her arms, her drab smock dark with blood.

The wolf saw her in the shadow and acknowledged her scent at the same instant. It was the unmistakable, bitter man-smell that meant danger, but tinged with an odor the wolf was tasting for the first time: the sweet, dusky odor of human blood.

His black lips curled back and his throat emitted a snarl. The gulls fled, and the sky was empty.

3.

The Meeting House

THE Reverend Adam Blakeman stood rigidly in the elevated pulpit, as if his spine were constructed of bog iron.

"It is a goodly land," he exclaimed. "Though full of wild beasts and savage men, it is a land where we may worship God with a true conscience. We have settled it with great difficulty and charge, and for love of Christ have we gladly endured its hardships and perils. And here, by His will, shall we thrive, on the good fare of brown bread and the Gospel!"

The Meeting House stood where the settlers had first landed at Sandy Hollow, a few yards from the river. It was a plain, square building of rough pine and oak logs, its chinks poorly insulated with moss and clay. There was no fireplace, and more than once in the cold, damp weeks of the first winter deadly blasts from the river had chilled the service. The communion bread had frozen and rattled in the plates.

Now, in the heat of midsummer, the same building retained the stifling air. No breezes brought relief, despite the invitation of an open door.

A small rustic tower on the roof held a bell that had been brought from Derbyshire, the first bell of the Connecticut Colony. It was rung lustily by Goodman Peake on the Sabbath and Lecture Days, and all agreed that its knell sounded more sweetly in the free air of America than it ever had across the sea.

24

The tower served as a lookout as well, with a clear view of the distant Sound, the mouth of the river, and the entire settlement—the stocks and whipping post in the grassy clearing below, the tidal mill just to the south, the rows of two-acre home-lots with their crudely thatched dwellings, then the ten-foot palisade.

Armed regulars sat in special seats just inside the narrow Meeting House door, and by general order, one male from each family was bearing arms. Muskets, swords, pistols, and powder horns clinked and clattered occasionally, as the men stretched their legs, arched their backs, and resettled themselves on the hard wooden benches.

The soldier on watch in the bell tower never worried about missing the sermon, for Reverend Blakeman's strident words rang out through the rafters.

"Oh, blessed be the God of Israel, who doth such wondrous things! The Lord was pleased to smite our enemies and give us this land for an inheritance; a land of beauty and abundance, of rich meadows and grand old forests; of fresh springs, rivers, ponds, and streams; of wild strawberries, raspberries, and blackberries; of shellfish, bluefish, shad, and bass; of turkeys, partridge, quail, geese, ducks, bear, and deer!"

A brassbound hourglass sat on a rough desk to the right of the pulpit, the white sand spilling freely into the bottom bulb. Thomas Hawley, the clerk, watched it anxiously, fighting the drowsiness brought on by the falling grains.

The moment the top bulb was empty, he stood up and came forward with much ceremony to invert the glass for the third time.

His move was received by a general rattling of weapons, but Reverend Blakeman ignored the hint. Today was his anniversary sermon, in celebration of the settlement's first year, and no one was more devoutly thankful than the Reverend himself.

"Even now," he continued, "as our corn flourishes in the Old

Field, we struggle to clear the roots and stumps for a New Field, in which to cultivate a future bounty and abundance. Oh, let us embrace the shining bosom of the land!"

His bushy eyebrows danced up and down. In the raised pulpit he appeared much taller than he was, a bearded giant in a short black frock coat.

The Reverend's sermons were notoriously long, but he was a talented preacher and a man of great piety, prudence, and learning.

When the sermon finally ended, Deacon Wells came forward to read out the Psalm, the Forty-fourth, chosen to reflect the Reverend's general theme:

> We have heard with our ears, O God, our fathers
> have told us, what work Thou didst in their days.

One by one the lines were recited and the congregation, without psalm books of their own, repeated them, singing off key:

> How Thou didst drive out the Heathen
> with They Hand!

Even as these words were repeated, reminding the settlers of the Great Pequot War, the soldier in the bell tower was marking the progress of a dugout canoe that had turned from the Sound into the mouth of the river.

The lone Red Man in its stern struggled against the current, digging his paddle into the ripples, left, then right. He kept close to the far bank, out of range of both voice and musket, the canoe riding unusually low in the water.

By the time the Psalms and final prayers were concluded, the canoe had passed out of sight to the north.

Then the congregation stood and Reverend Blakeman exited,

as stiff as a steeple, arm in arm with his wife, to receive their respectful greetings outside.

The men followed from the benches to the left of the aisle, the women from the benches to the right, according to their rank and station: Philip Groves, the ruling elder; William Hopkins, the first magistrate; old Nicolas Knell, deputy to the General Court of Connecticut; Thomas Fairchild, the prominent merchant whose ancestors had fought in the Crusades; Thomas Hawley, the clerk.

Next came John Hurd, the miller; William Beardsley, the mason; and Jon Thomson, who had brought fruit trees from Leicestershire. Then Richard Harvey, the tailor, and the linen weaver, William Wilcockson.

Sergeant Nichols was absent, making his guard rounds along the palisade.

Moses Wheeler, a ship's carpenter, came last. He always seated himself in the back of the Meeting House, though his sister Jane was married to Reverend Blakeman. The burly man had a habit of swearing loudly at the least provocation, and his presence in the rear helped Sexton Peake keep the children in order.

Among the women, only Goody Thomson seemed imperfectly seated—closer to the front than the station of a poor yeoman's spouse allowed. But Goody Blakeman had taken her under wing and none dared argue with the Reverend's wife.

The Widow Paine had voluntarily placed herself in front of the children. She sat directly across from Moses Wheeler, whose boisterous nature reminded her of her lost husband.

Despite their social rank, necessity made the women equals. They were cooks, laundresses, soap and candle makers, tailoresses, dressmakers, and shirtmakers, their long days of carding wool and rotting flax followed by days of spinning and weaving. Only on Sabbath and lecture days could the women show their place.

There were twenty families altogether, all plainly dressed. The women wore long dresses despite the heat, their hair bound and hid by simple caps. The men wore breeches and stockings, with open shirts or unadorned waistcoats.

They exited slowly, followed by the restless children in the last few rows. Young John Blakeman, one of the Reverend's six children, was heartbroken. Ruth had not been in her seat.

His father had noticed, too. "What? Young Ruth not keeping the Sabbath?" He spoke loudly, his bushy eyebrows touching.

The Widow Paine halted abruptly by the stocks and whipping post, already on her way home. She was a short, stout woman, said to be sixty years old.

"The child is ill," she called back, thrusting her fists deep into the pockets of her wrinkled apron. "I am in hope she may attend this afternoon."

Goody Blakeman strained her neck above the congregation, her voice as harsh as a nutmeg grater. "Woe to the idle shepherd that leaveth the flock!" She was a proud, attractive woman, an inch or two taller than her husband, and inclined to take his duty for her own.

Moses Wheeler shouted from the door of the Meeting House. "Now, sister, surely thine own six children are enough for one woman to attend to!"

Old Nicolas Knell, an elfish man with a long white beard, cackled.

"And who shall tend to *thee*, dear brother?" Goody Blakeman rejoined. "We hear thou takest a barrel of cider for a drinking cup!"

Moses Wheeler roared, his broad hands on his belly. "We Puritans are not as severe as thou would'st have us believe. We like the drink but despise the drunkard."

"Aye," said Nicolas Knell. "Amen to that!"

"Pray, brother, that thou walk a straight line to the afternoon meeting!"

Moses Wheeler roared again, joined by several other men,

the women turning to one another with scandalous glances. In the grassy clearing by the stocks, the Widow Paine's eyes crinkled in delight.

"Enough!" Reverend Blakeman entreated, his bushy eyebrows separating as he grinned. "Such idle chatter will addle the brains of the children."

The congregation filed by, and he offered his hand.

"Your goodwife is an inspiration to us all," Goody Thomson said. "My Jon and I hope for more children, to be as fruitful as thee and thy Jane!"

Sexton Peake, switch in hand, herded the last few children from the Meeting House and trotted off after the Widow Paine. He was a small, nervous man, whom the children delighted in irritating.

"I, for one, did not mind Ruth's absence," he said, once he had caught up, "though I am ashamed to admit it. All good Christian souls belong at Meeting, but she sets the others to laughing, sticking out her infernal tongue."

Widow Paine set her hands on her wide hips, large hands that could swing an ax and chop wood by the cord. "It's but her way of considering. The tongue goes out—"

"—and the Devil goes in!" Sexton Peake finished for her.

"Put up thy stick and go strike the bell, Goodman Peake, and may it ring some sense into your head!" Widow Paine stalked off.

Goodman Peake arched his willow switch, grasping it tightly at each end as if lecturing the children. "Is it true what they say, Widow Paine, that the child is not of thy flesh?"

Widow Paine whirled and raised a fist. "Wicked hearsay, sir! I came late to childbearing. It were the Lord's will. But for my dead Jonas, thou would'st be rotting in Massachusetts Bay!"

Turning her back, the Widow Paine hurried away, burdened by the truth behind the rumor. "Common knowledge, is it?" she muttered aloud. "The work of Goody Blakeman, no doubt! She bears her pride like she bears her children—excessively! 'Be fruitful and multiply,' says she. It be stitched across her proud breast. She would have us always pregnant, as our duty. 'Poor Goody Thomson, only two children!' One would think her barren with only two!"

Barren. Widow Paine despised the word as well as the reality. But she feared only for Ruth's sake.

She crossed the corner of the Blakemans' home-lot, twice the size of the others and closest to the Meeting House. Three large pines had been left standing as a windbreak. Behind the middle one young John Blakeman waited, having circled from the congregation at top speed.

"Widow Paine," he whispered breathlessly. "Wait!"

"What, will the pines chide me too?"

"It is I, Master John." The tall youth stepped from the trees, holding a pine cone behind his back. "I—will she come this afternoon, Widow Paine?"

"Aye, child, I trust she will."

"It were a serious matter, not keeping the Sabbath."

"More serious to swoon in such heat and disturb us all, although I know a young lad who would gladly carry a girl to the river to take the air."

John Blakeman blushed and held out the pine cone, his cuffs too short for his wrists.

"It's for Ruth. She pretends to smoke them and amuses us."

Widow Paine shook a fat finger. "Such abetting will not amuse thy father! He'll have you locked in yonder stocks!" She put out her hand and took the pine cone. "Now be off to thy brothers and sisters!"

In the Meeting House tower, the soldier who had seen the lone Red Man was relieved by another guard.

4.

Nimrod

RUTH opened her eyes slowly, blinked several times, and squinted straight up at the sky. The sun was somewhere to her right. White clouds drifted high overhead against a canopy of royal blue. One of the clouds resembled a bell.

Was she dreaming?

The sweet, soft tolling of a bell seemed to linger on the outer edges of her consciousness.

Droplets of cool water splashed her lightly in the face, flashing briefly in rainbow prisms before they struck. She felt very tired, confined in the heat.

The water droplets came again. She studied the clouds. It was not raining, nor were the clouds moving, although they appeared to be drifting left to right.

No, it was she who was moving. She was floating, barely conscious, except now she could recognize the sound of a distant bell. And she could feel the push and swell of the river beneath her.

Water droplets sprayed her again. Ruth braced herself in the bow of the canoe. At her feet lay a wolf, its eyes glassy, jaws open, large red tongue draped to the side. Dried blood caked the black rim of its mouth. A feathered shaft stuck up from its shoulder at an awkward angle. The large yellow eyes said nothing.

The water droplets came again, glinting in the sunlight. The flat blade of a paddle—cutting left, then right—flicked the water forward with every other stroke. The Red Man who held it was naked to the waist. He wore buckskin leggings, and his moccasin-clad feet rested against the rump of the wolf. His hair, as black as a kettle, was pulled back severely and bound in a short pigtail above the right ear. A small leather pouch hung from a thong around his neck, inscribed with the letter N.

His eyes were dark and, like the wolf's, said nothing.

At times, as he worked his paddle effortlessly, the Red Man seemed to Ruth no older than young John Blakeman. Other times, when he looked over his shoulder or squinted into the sun, the lines tightened about his eyes and he seemed immensely old.

Beneath the narrow bench on which he sat lay a hickory bow, a quiver of arrows, a flint knife, and a long stem pipe with a stone bowl.

The canoe moved at mid-river, headed straight upstream. No need now to keep to the far shore, dodging overhanging branches and slick black rocks. The way was clear and progress was steady, despite the heavy load.

Ruth reclined uncomfortably, knees apart. Her smock had been slit along each leg and tied beneath her like a breechclout. She could still feel the cramps in her abdomen, but they were secondary to the pain in her leg. Her left thigh was purple and swollen from the wolf wound. The punctures bled freely. The crush of jaws had missed the bone.

Before long, when the trees along the shore gave way to a brief meadow, the Red Man pointed the canoe in. Jumping from the stern in shallow water, he dragged the bow onto a short stretch of beach.

Ruth's leg throbbed as the spine of the canoe crunched on the gravel. She closed her eyes, some of the day's events coming back to her. Her wound, however, and the brute animal at her feet were still a mystery.

Cupping his hands, the Red Man poured cool water over her

thigh, washing the blood to the bottom of the canoe. Then he disappeared into the meadow, and Ruth slept.

When she woke, the Red Man was standing over her with a fistful of yarrow—strong-scented clusters of pink and white flowers and finely toothed green leaves.

Discarding the flowers, the Red Man plucked the leaves from the stems and folded them, bruising them gently in his fingertips until they produced a thin juice. Applying the liquid to each puncture, he soon halted the bleeding.

He worked quickly and quietly, never once looking up. The remaining yarrow stalks were dropped at Ruth's feet, where large flies crawled in the mouth of the wolf.

Cupping his hands in the river again, the Red Man held forth water for Ruth to drink. When she refused it, he drank himself.

He refilled his hands. This time Ruth accepted the water, drinking hastily as the Red Man stared upstream.

Then the canoe was in the river again, gliding noiselessly through the ripples, and the gentle nudging lulled Ruth back to sleep.

The river had narrowed, no more than a hundred yards wide. Tall pines on the bank blocked the sun now, their long shadows reaching to mid-stream. The Red Man kept the canoe well within them.

Toward dusk Ruth woke suddenly as the canoe was dragged ashore, the bottom grating on small stones. The bumping shot sharp pains through her thigh.

Leaving the canoe, the Red Man slipped along the shore, fanning his hand in a curious movement beneath the overhanging branches. In the dim light Ruth watched him. She was conscious only of the throbbing in her leg.

When the Red Man returned, his hand was sticky with cobwebs. Peeling them off, he twisted them into slender plugs, which he packed into the punctures of her wound. Ruth winced, expecting more pain, but the pain did not come.

Then the Red Man placed her hands on the gunwale, motioning for her to rise. Bracing herself, she tried to stand, but the loss of blood and the pain in her leg made her weak. She collapsed back into the bow.

The Red Man placed her hands on the gunwale again.

Favoring her good leg, Ruth stood shakily. The Red Man turned, bent forward, and patted himself on the shoulder. Ruth hesitated, then put her arms around his neck and was quickly lifted from the canoe.

A few yards upstream a narrow path led away from the river to a grassy clearing surrounded by large pines. In the center was a shallow, rock-lined pit. On the far side, lower branches had been cut away from the trees, forming a natural cave with an overhanging roof. Depositing Ruth inside on a bed of pine needles, the Red Man returned to the river. He pushed the canoe out of sight among the brush and tree roots, then brought his own things back to the clearing.

Striking his flint knife against a stone in the pit, he started a small fire with twigs and dry grass. As the flames caught, he added more wood.

When the fire was blazing several feet in the air, the Red Man broke off a pine bough and wet it in the river. Placing it over the flames and withdrawing it quickly, he sent a round puff of gray smoke into the early evening sky. Soon the puffs rose regularly, dissolving high above, leaving no trace of their message.

Their gentle, patient rising had a calming effect on Ruth. She watched the smoke quietly, trying to piece together what had happened to her.

Then the Red Man tossed the branch aside, and darkness closed in overhead. The fire blazed in the pit. Somewhere beyond the clearing, a noisy brook ran to meet the river downstream.

The Red Man ducked under the pine branches and knelt before Ruth. *"Mogke-oaas,"* he said, speaking for the first time.

Ruth could only stare.

"Mogke-oaas," he repeated.

Ruth studied his face. Away from the firelight, she could no longer distinguish the different color of his skin.

She shook her head helplessly in response to his words. The Red Man crawled out from beneath the pine branches and left the clearing.

An owl hooted in the woods. The distant brook seemed noisier. Keeping her leg still, Ruth lay back on the soft pine needles. A mosquito lighted on her arm and she brushed it away. Presently, she could hear the Red Man returning, his footsteps heavier than before.

Entering the clearing, he stood before the fire. The wolf was slung over his back, its tail hanging to the ground. In the firelight, the large yellow eyes seemed alive.

The Red Man rolled the huge animal to the ground, put his foot on its back, and yanked the feathered shaft from its shoulder. Tossing it aside, he took up his knife.

A brilliant full moon had risen overhead. Within the clearing, it suddenly seemed like day. Wide awake, Ruth watched the Red Man as he went to work by the fire.

Inserting his knife below the wolf's lower jaw, he sliced the fur straight down past the stomach and out the tail. With a quick movement of his wrist he carved a ring above each paw. Then he slit along the back of the hind legs, joining each incision to the first long cut.

He did the same for the front legs, extending the cuts to the lower jaw.

Working patiently, with the same care he had bestowed on Ruth, he carved the skin about the eyes, nose, and mouth, cutting the ears close to the head. Knife and hand moved deftly in and around the massive, frozen jaws.

The wolf, to Ruth, still looked formidable. It was only when the Red Man began to peel away the hide that the animal no longer seemed a threat.

Grasping the skin with both hands, he worked it down the hind legs, then over the rump and off the tail bone. Using his thumbnail, he nudged it along the spine, separating it from the ribs and shoulders. Next he worked it away from the front legs, pausing to wipe his fingers in the grass. Finally, with a quick yank, he ripped the skin over the skull.

The Red Man held the skin at arm's length, then sat down and draped it across his knees. Using the edge of his knife, he scraped away the surplus fat from the soft, moist underside, depositing the yellowish globules on a flat rock beside him. There was no blood on the pelt. The incisions had been perfect—not too shallow, not too deep.

When all the fat had been removed, the skin, fur-side down, was spread on the matted grass. The Red Man turned to the carcass.

Lifting a large round rock from the edge of the fire, he dashed in the skull. White brains spilled from the fracture. A quick slit with the knife opened the wolf's belly and, reaching within, the Red Man removed the dark liver. Tossing it on the flat rock with the fat globules, he added the brains and chopped the whole into a spongy mixture.

Taking a fistful with each hand, he worked it vigorously into the underside of the pelt.

Something about the way he was working reminded Ruth of the Widow Paine. For the first time, panic seized her—for herself and for those at Sandy Hollow. How long had she been gone? A few hours? A few days? Again she tried to make sense of it all, to grasp her present situation. She could only watch.

Spreading the pelt again, the Red Man added a bundle of dry grass to the center, folded in the corners, and wrapped it into a soft, solid ball. Then he set it aside.

He moved to the carcass again. Grabbing the forelegs, he dragged it into the fire.

Instantly the flames leaped higher, licking the dim space overhead, sizzling and spitting with grease. The Red Man watched intently, his eyes dark and unmoving. At length he came to Ruth beneath the canopy of pines. *"Mogke-oaas,"* he said, as if to himself, and sat beside her.

The moon had risen to the center of the hole above the trees. Occasionally a bat flitted from the shadows across the pale light of the clearing. The flames consumed the carcass hungrily, sending up white smoke and a sharp, burnt odor.

Ruth lay in the pine needles and gazed at the fire. She felt weak, unable to sleep. Again and again in the flames she saw the shell heap, her name in the sand, and . . . what had happened then?

She turned to the Red Man, but he was absorbed by the fire. After a while, he got up and left the pine cave to sharpen his flint against a rock.

Sparks flew from the blade. When his knife was keen again, he raised the carcass from the fire and sliced a large piece of meat from the rump. Cutting it in half, he returned to the pine shelter and extended a portion to Ruth.

The greasy smell made her nauseous and she turned her head.

The Red Man spoke sharply. *"Mogke-oaas!"*

Meekly, Ruth accepted the burnt slab. Taking a small bite, she found it stringy and tough, like oily venison. She chewed it quickly and forced herself to swallow, then set the remainder beside her.

The Red Man did not object. Devouring his own piece, he seemed satisfied that Ruth had eaten. When he finished, he left the shelter again and dragged the blackened carcass from the flames to the far edge of the clearing.

Taking up his pipe, he filled it from the pouch at his chest, lit it with a flaming twig, and sat cross-legged before the fire, the carcass at arm's length to his left. Without fuel, the fire soon died away, leaving only the red glow of embers. The air reeked of wolf flesh, an oily stench that seemed to permeate the matted grass and pine branches, spreading out far from the river into the woods beyond.

An owl hooted, answered by another, and Ruth watched the Red Man smoke his pipe. He sat absolutely still, pipe in hand, its thin smoke rising into the moonlight. His eyes never left the dying embers. He seemed expectant, patient, alert.

Ruth's stomach gurgled, complaining of hunger. Reluctantly she took up the wolf meat. Brushing off the pine needles, she forced herself to eat it and forget about her wound. By the time she had finished, the moon had left the opening above the clearing. For the first time, they were in total darkness.

The fire died out. The summer night descended. Ruth listened to her heartbeat, its pulse echoing in her thigh. She seemed to float, dreamily, in the pine boughs overhead, leaving her body in the soft needles below.

The Red Man didn't appear to breathe at all. He was sitting as still as the stones that lined the pit at his feet.

The air seemed to ring as the night slipped away, long minutes turning into hours. A faint dampness set in, chilling the ground, and the Red Man sat by the dead fire, smoking his pipe. Ruth rolled over, unconscious of her wound. Had she slept?

The Red Man refilled his pipe. The scent of wolf meat had given way to pine sap. Then, through the misty darkness, just as Ruth was lapsing again into sleep, she thought she heard the Red Man whisper, *"Mogke-oaas."*

He laid his pipe aside. Ruth sat straight up, trembling.

The Red Man turned his gaze from the dead fire to the carcass. Placing his right hand beside his ear, he raised his middle and index fingers to form a V, and brought his hand slowly forward. Then he folded his arms firmly across his chest.

Above the carcass at the edge of the clearing, a pair of yellow eyes appeared, embedded in the ghostly fog of vague, gray fur.

The animal had traveled for miles, drawn by the smell of burnt flesh. He fixed the Red Man in an unblinking stare.

The Red Man returned the stare, intense, determined, pure. His muscles tightened, but he didn't move. Delicate information, Ruth suddenly realized, was being exchanged as man and wolf studied each other. The wolf had come for his kin, as the Red Man knew he must.

The wordless communication continued, the eyes penetrating each other, devoid of feeling. The night was at its blackest, the chilled air clean and sharp, and there was no misunderstanding.

The decision, when finally reached, was mutual. A respectful truce. *Let us walk as brothers of the forest.*

Then the gray wolf dragged the carcass from the clearing.

5.

Captain Mason

As the final pealing of the bell for the afternoon service lingered on the stifling air, Mary Nichols turned in her place ever so slightly to steal a glance over her shoulder.

The Meeting House door stood wide open, but her husband, Sergeant Francis Nichols, was not yet seated. He had gone to set the guard along the palisade.

Ruth was still missing, and the Widow Paine was missing, too. "Ahem!"

Goody Thomson cleared her throat, her chastising eyes finding those of Mary Nichols from beneath the wide brim of her cap.

Mary Nichols faced front immediately and folded her hands in her lap. "Patience!" she told herself. How she wished to be as brave as her husband, as peppery and harsh when need be! Instead, she found herself in a constant turmoil whenever duty took him from her side.

"Patience!" she told herself again.

Inverting the brassbound hourglass with a loud thump, Goodman Hawley brought an end to her fretting. The congregation rose as Reverend Blakeman re-entered swiftly. They had just finished an hour of rest and a midday meal of pork pie, cheese, and brown bread. Ahead lay three hours of lecturing, prayers, and psalms.

Mr. Blakeman's bushy eyebrows danced fervently as he ascended the pulpit, eager to continue in worship, but the con-

40

gregation had scarcely reseated itself when Widow Paine burst through the doorway.

"The girl is missing!" she cried. "I have looked everywhere! My Ruth is gone!"

The regulars restrained her as the congregation turned in confusion. Only Goody Thomson remained facing the pulpit until Goody Blakeman herself stood to gaze at the commotion.

Moses Wheeler jumped up on his bench in front of the children, his head almost in the rafters. "By God's blood, unhand the woman! Let us go to search at once!" He ignored the sharp glare that was shot his way by his sister from the first row.

"Brother!" Jane Blakeman squeaked. "Remember where thou art!"

The Reverend pounded his fist on the pulpit. "Sit ye down, everyone! Halt this hue and cry! Anna Paine, please come forward!"

Shaking loose from the guard in the doorway, Widow Paine stomped up the aisle, fists jammed deep in the pocket of her apron. "My Ruth is gone from her bed, sir! She may be in danger!"

Reverend Blakeman had no chance to answer. Sergeant Nichols flew in the door. "The postern gate is found open! All armed men outside!"

Mary Nichols fainted straight away, slumping to the packed dirt floor. Moses Wheeler jumped down from his bench and headed for the doorway. "It be Ruth, then, who has left!"

"What? Ruth gone?"

"Francis, did ye see her on thy rounds?"

"I stopped at thy dwellin' as ye requested, Anna Paine. It were mid-mornin' and the girl were on her pallet. There were a loaded musket on the table."

"Aye, as I left it, just in case."

Reverend Blakeman raised his arm. "Let us pray for her safe return!"

"No, father!" young John Blakeman shouted. "Let us go to search!"

Goody Blakeman spoke sharply. "Keep thyself within the palisade, John Blakeman!"

"Oh, mother!"

The Reverend pounded his fist again. "Possess thy souls in patience!" He stared hard and long at his son. "Sergeant Nichols!" he ordered finally. "Form a party of the men outside! Women and children to remain here! May the good Lord—"

His remaining words were lost in the clatter of arms as the meeting dissolved. The regulars were already on the riverbank with Moses Wheeler. Sergeant Nichols followed in a crush of men, young John Blakeman at their heels.

Widow Paine hurried out behind them, Reverend Blakeman steering her up the aisle by the shoulders.

Jane Blakeman waved a hand. "Remember, Anna, there be some spiritual advantage in every adversity!"

Goody Thomson shook her head in disgust. "No doubt the girl's off to the meadow fetching lady slippers!"

"Hush, dear!" Jane Blakeman scolded. "Attend to poor Mary Nichols. Children, take thy seats! Oh, Sexton, where is thy switch?"

Outside, Widow Paine elbowed her way through the crowd surrounding Sergeant Nichols. He was issuing instructions, dividing the men.

"Fairchild and Hawley, try along the river! Wilcockson and Hurd, out the north gate and south along the palisade! Beardsley and Thomson, work north from the postern gate! Moses and I will search the Old Field and beyond!"

"And I," said Nicolas Knell, his voice cackling, "shall watch over the women and children. Thou'rt all more swift of foot than I."

"Sexton Peake and Deacon Wells shall aid thee. Keep everyone here!" One of the regulars had climbed from the bell tower and was about to descend. "And you there," Sergeant Nichols yelled to him, "keep to the lookout!"

As the men scattered in all directions, Widow Paine caught Sergeant Nichols by the arm. "Did ye speak with Ruth this morning?"

"Aye, Anna. We spoke briefly of London when I looked in. Shops and carriages—the usual things—but she weren't so keen on listenin'. She said she wished to sleep. She were in a strange mood, so I went on my way."

"Lend me thy sword," Reverend Blakeman interrupted, "and cock thy pistol! Beware of ambush. The savages may have a hand!"

Sergeant Nichols unbuckled his scabbard and rushed off after the others.

Widow Paine clasped her hands to her face, her wide eyes brimming with tears. "I'll myself check the home-lots again, sir. She has a way of wandering about the home-lots."

"Take my John with thee," the Reverend offered, but young John Blakeman was nowhere to be seen.

By late afternoon, the feeling of crisis at the Meeting House had been replaced by a general weariness. The children, still on their benches, answered in grunts and monotones as Deacon Wells tried to drill them on the Reverend's morning sermon. The searchers had not returned.

Each time Mr. Wells raised his eyes to the open door, the children spun about in their seats. But there was only Sexton Peake behind them, tapping his switch in the palm of his hand. The women kept to the front benches, talking guardedly.

Goody Thomson stared at the hourglass on the desk to the right of the pulpit. She was a plain woman who liked to be seen in the company of Goody Blakeman, as if the latter's beauty enhanced her own. Her thick, dark frown made her ugly. "It is well beyond the hour of worship," she complained. "There be kettles to wash and stockings to mend and water to fetch from the spring."

"Hush, dear," Jane Blakeman scolded. "It is not too late for prayer. Mary Nichols! Will ye eat thine own fingers?"

Mary Nichols heaved a nervous sigh, her mouth drooping at the corners, then she buried her head in her hands, worried about her Francis.

Suddenly the sentinel in the bell tower stomped on the roof, startling all below. "A sail! A ship in the harbor!"

The Meeting House instantly emptied. Woman and children raced to the riverbank, chasing Sexton Peake and Deacon Wells. Old Nicholas Knell was already at the wharf, tugging on his long white beard and dancing about like a leprechaun. "A brigantine!" he squealed. "A proper brig!"

Up the wide mouth of the Pootatuck on the high flood tide came a square-rigged, two-masted ship, the first in the year since the settlers had arrived. In the absence of a good breeze, its sheets hung flat and wrinkled.

Thoughts of crisis turned to thoughts of joy—of bolts of cloth, kegs of nails, ironware, and woolen blankets; of kitchen utensils and muskets; even books. But it was soon apparent that the ship was not from England, not even from Massachusetts Bay Colony. It was flying the blue colors of Connecticut, having come from Hartford down the Connecticut River.

Too large to dock at the crude log wharf that Moses Wheeler had built in the cove of Sandy Hollow, the brig anchored in mid-river. A tiny dinghy soon put ashore. In the bow stood Captain John Mason.

He was a tall, portly man—as big as Moses Wheeler—with a ragged beard gray before its time. In 1635, he had helped to organize the Connecticut Colony. When the Great Pequot War began soon after, the General Court appointed him Chief Commander of the amassed Colonial Forces. The Great Pequot War had made him a hero.

His large brown eyes flashed with curiosity as he stalked away from the wharf. The waiting crowd of women and children puzzled him. "Where is thy Reverend?" he enquired of Nicolas Knell. "For the sake of the preachings of that worthy man, if I had my choice, I would choose to live and die under the ministry of Mr. Blakeman!"

Before Nicolas Knell could answer, the Captain had left him behind with huge strides.

As Sexton Peake and Deacon Wells hurried to greet the visitor, Reverend Blakeman himself appeared, returning from the search. He raised high the sword he was carrying. "We saw thy sails, Captain! Thou'rt timely arrived!"

Captain Mason smiled broadly. "We ought to have been in harbor yesterday, sir, but were victims of fickle winds. Yet I assure you, Mr. Blakeman, though we sailed on the Sabbath, our duties were rightly observed!" He extended his brawny arm and shook the Reverend's hand vigorously.

Captain Mason gazed about Sandy Hollow, his eyes roving from the Meeting House, to the tide mill, to the dwellings on the home-lots. "Ye have carved a proper home for God in the wilderness, sir. I applaud thy work on behalf of the General Court!"

Reverend Blakeman replied solemnly, "I fear thy visit finds us in the midst of tribulation."

"What's amiss?" Captain Mason's large brown eyes grew bold.

"The young girl called Ruth Paine, either kidnapped or stolen away. And if fled, then captured or lost. Since the morning prayer, it seems. Her father, Jonas Paine, you will recall, died in thy—"

"Aye, as we crushed the heathen Pequot. I remember him well and the sacrifice he made."

The two men paused as Joseph Hawley and Thomas Fairchild appeared below the tidal mill, making their way back upriver.

Then Wilcockson and Hurd, with downcast eyes, came across the Blakemans' home-lot. Beardsley and Thomson came out of the woods to join them.

Reverend Blakeman squinted at the huge red sun sitting on the jagged edge of the palisade. "It seems thy colors have called us home, Captain. We have searched in vain since noon. It will soon be too dark to look further."

Captain Mason spoke again. "I come on business, sir, with orders from the General Court. Sergeant Nichols is to form a trainband, to exercise the men of Sandy Hollow in military discipline. But I correct myself, sir—the men of 'Stratford,' for such are ye now called in the Record, after Stratford-Upon-Avon in England!"

If not for Ruth, the news would have been met with shouts of joy. The settlers still had strong feelings for England.

"But where *is* Sergeant Nichols?" Captain Mason surveyed the crowd of men around him.

"At the bluffs, sir!" Moses Wheeler called. He came swiftly through the grassy clearing to join the others. "Too far to see thy sails. God's blood, we could have used thee earlier!"

Reverend Blakeman tapped his sword against his leg. "Is Anna Paine returned?"

"She rests at her dwelling, sir." Squeezing in between Moses Wheeler and Captain Mason, old Nicolas Knell made his report. "The worry is too much for her. And Mary Nichols be out of sorts, too. She needs looking after, I fear."

"Let us gather at the Meeting House." Reverend Blakeman pointed his sword at Sexton Peake. "Send the women and children home. Do ye bring other news, Captain Mason?"

"The Pequannocks neglect their tribute, sir. They fail to send the agreed upon wampum. Though they be not hostile like the former Pequots, we are forced to remind them of our signed agreements respecting the land." Captain Mason looked to the brig. "We come also to survey the western bounds of Stratford, so the Pequannocks—and future settlers—will know and respect them."

Sexton Peake had turned from the group and was hurrying to the Meeting House, waving his switch overhead. "Women and children are dismissed! Ruth is not found! The men will meet within!"

The women and children milled about, eager for news. Deacon Wells, following the sexton, hastened to disperse them. "No apparent danger! Women and children to return home!"

Jane Blakeman ignored the orders, studying the crowd that approached with her husband. Suddenly she stepped forth and shouted, "Where is my John! Adam, is he not with the men?"

Reverend Blakeman stopped short and looked about him. "What? Is our John not returned?"

But worry had no chance to run its course. Young John Blakeman hastened out of the dusk by the stocks and whipping post, hands cupped against his chest as if carrying potatoes. Sergeant Nichols ran breathlessly not far behind.

"Here I am, father! I have found Ruth's name at the bluffs! It were writ in shells and there be blood upon them!"

The small group of settlers fell silent. One of the younger children began to cry. Captain Mason pointed Reverend Blakeman to the Meeting House as the sun dropped behind the palisade.

6.

Thomas Stanton

IN her sleep, Ruth heard a wolf howling and she dreamed of a silver wolf with its head thrown back, howling to a full silver moon. The sound began as a single note, rising sharply as the animal strained for volume, a long, loud, throaty howl that broke off abruptly at the end.

Ruth had heard wolves howl in the night before, their cries piercing the palisade at Sandy Hollow. The sound had stiffened the hair on her scalp and prickled her skin. Not even Widow Paine's warm hand on her shoulder could make her feel safe.

But this howl, filling the blackness of the forest and the immense midnight sky, seemed a part of the darkness, like the brook beyond the clearing or the pine needles on which she lay. It was neither hostile nor friendly. It was simply there, distinct and clear.

In her sleep, Ruth heard voices as well. One of them belonged to the Red Man, solemn and low, with words she did not understand. The other was in English, the speaker unknown, its tone also solemn and low. The voices answered each other rhythmically—strange Indian words translated into English—causing Ruth to dream of Deacon Wells reading the Psalms.

"The land is a mother that never dies."

"Let me be like *mogke-oaas*, the great animal."

A small fire burned in the pit as Ruth slept. The long stem pipe with the stone bowl passed slowly back and forth between the two men, glowing like an ember. The wolf howled again, as if it had been listening."

"Before the White Man, peaceful was before me, behind me, under me, over me, all around me."

"With all beings and all things we were as relatives."

"The land, all of it, belonged to us."

"We lived off the animals of the forest."

"We lived off the fruits and wild berries."

"We lived off the eels in the river."

"We lived off the shellfish in the Sound."

"Our feasts were ancient and sacred."

"We piled high the bone mounds, the shell mounds."

Ruth rolled over in the pine needles, her memory stirring, her wounded leg as heavy as a boulder. What was it? What was this dream?

The silver wolf's howl split the stars.

"This is the fire that will help the generations to come, if it is used in a sacred manner."

"If it is not, it will do great harm."

"Let me be like *mogke-oaas*, the great animal."

When Ruth woke, the sun stood directly overhead, filling the hole where the trees met the sky. Beneath the pine branches it was dim and cool, the light entering in broad, slanted shafts. The clearing seemed much smaller than it had in the darkness.

A small black kettle hung from a tripod of sticks above a fire in the pit. The wolf pelt lay staked in the grass to stretch and dry, its oiled underside to the sun.

Insects buzzed nearby and the brook crashed its way through the woods. The Red Man was nowhere to be seen.

Ruth rubbed her eyes. Her long nose felt cold, and the knot in her smock was damp with blood.

She stared at her thigh. The swelling was down, but there were pink welts above each of the four fang holes. Her leg was stiff and sore.

Where was the Red Man? she wondered. Where had the kettle come from? There had been no kettle in the canoe, and now there was a kettle boiling over the fire.

As she studied it, Ruth realized how hungry she was. One thing was certain: she would eat no more wolf meat. Its taste was still rancid in her mouth. And the wolf meat had made her have strange dreams.

Dragging herself from the pine shelter, she crawled into the dry heat of the clearing. The bright sun stung her eyes. A large pine cone in the grass brought an image of the Reverend's son—that lanky, awkward, blond-headed John Blakeman.

Why, Ruth thought, did he tease her so? And why, when teased, did she perform, smoking pine cones and clucking like a chicken? It seemed so stupid, especially now, away from Sandy Hollow.

Sandy Hollow! The thought distressed her. She hoped Widow Paine would have more sense than to worry. She had never worried at the trading post in Windsor whenever Ruth ran off to the woods.

How to let Widow Paine know she was safe? It was something to pray for, she knew that for a fact. But the words wouldn't come.

As for the others—well, the others could be hanged! What had they made of her but a clown? Reverend Blakeman had offered a promise of well-being and safety in the community because Papa Paine had died in the Great Pequot War. Papa Paine had died to make Sandy Hollow possible, but the Puritan life there seemed no match for life at Windsor.

Ruth curled her tongue to her nose. Though she had been injured, she wasn't sorry for her excursion on the Sabbath. She had felt free outside the palisade.

A twig snapped in the woods behind the clearing, and she looked up quickly. Fear gripped her. Someone was coming, someone noisier than the Red Man. She couldn't run; her leg wouldn't bear it. All she could do was sit in the grass and wait.

"Who's there?" she shouted finally.

Presently a tall, thin man made his way through the trees, pushing away the pine branches before him. He held a black felt hat against his waist, a sharp gray feather stuck in its beaded band. Like the Red Man, he wore buckskin leggings and moccasins. His linsey-woolsey shirt was threadbare, open at the neck to reveal gray hairs on his chest. Short white whiskers grew across his cheeks, connecting a black moustache with his salt-and-pepper sideburns. His balding head gleamed in the sunlight.

"Well, little sister," he said cheerily. "Sleepin' to high noon like a lady of London! It's about time you were up and about yer chores!" The man crossed to the kettle and peeked in. "Ah! Just about done! Breakfast for you, my dear; lunch for old Tom."

Ruth smiled and sat up straight. "What's to eat?" she asked warily. "I'll be having no more wolf meat!"

"The wolf is gone," the man said soberly. "We've got an eel in the pot. Here." He held out his hat and took a few steps toward Ruth. "Have some berries in the meanwhile. I just picked 'em in the woods. Blackberries and raspberries, right in season. Go on, now, don't be bashful. The name's Stanton. Thomas Stanton. I'm the Indian interpreter in these parts."

Setting his hat in the grass where Ruth could reach it, Thomas Stanton returned to the kettle and began to stir the steaming water with a long, bone-handled knife.

Ruth took a fistful of berries and pressed them into her mouth. They were soft, ripe, and sweet. Their juices ran through her fingers. "I be Ruth," she said with a mouthful.

"Aye, from the plantation at Cupheag."

"We call it Sandy Hollow."

"Do ye now?"

Ruth looked up. "And where do *you* come from?"

"Down the Pootatuck in my skiff by last night's moon, as soon as I saw yer smoke."

"What happened to—"

"Nimrod? Gone now, about his business. He saved yer life, little sister. That wolf"—Thomas Stanton gestured with his knife to the outstretched pelt—"were dead before he ever clamped his jaws about yer leg. Quite a lucky lady, I'd say, that Nimrod were passin' by."

"Nimrod?" Ruth wiped her hand in the matted grass, remembering the N on the Red Man's leather pouch. "But that be a Christian name. From Genesis: 'He was a mighty hunter before the Lord.'"

"They have taught ye well at Sandy Hollow."

"Deacon Wells makes us recite everything a hundred times!"

"So do Nimrod! He had me repeat everythin' he told me last night, so he could hear how it would sound in English, even though he couldn't understand a word. He's a Pequannock, made a Christian after the Pequot War—one of the few who were spared because he hadn't shed any English blood. He had a reputation for huntin' so he were christened Nimrod on the spot."

"Reverend Blakeman says all Red Men are devils."

Stanton halted his long knife in midair above the kettle and stared into the boiling water. His shirt was covered with stickers and burrs from foraging in the woods. Wrinkles formed across his brow, all the more prominent because of his baldness.

"When an Indian maiden enters womanhood," he said finally, "the Pequannocks say *she has seen the wolf*." He pointed again with his knife to the wolf pelt. "You, little sister, have taken 'em at their word!"

Ruth straightened her legs, embarrassed by the knot in her smock, then lowered her eyes to the black hat beside her in the grass. The gray feather stuck in the beaded band was that of an eagle. The magnificent eagle had been her Papa's favorite bird.

"Reverend Blakeman says that wolves are devils, too." Wiping her hand in the grass again, Ruth helped herself to more berries.

Stanton shook his head. "Yer Indians and wolves are similar," he said. "They both come and go in the night. They stare from the edge of fields and make you uneasy. And they both have powerful hearin'. An Indian can put his ear to the ground and hear yer footsteps comin'. A wolf can hear a cow chewin' its cud. The Pequannocks say a wolf can hear clouds passin' overhead."

Then, putting a hand to his ear, the bald-headed man raised two fingers to form a *V* and brought his hand slowly forward. "Both yer Indians and wolves use sign language."

"Nimrod made that sign!"

"It is the sign of the wolf," Stanton said.

"Mocky-oats?"

"*Mogke-oaas*. The great animal."

Ruth reached into the hat for more berries.

"Indians and wolves respect each other," Stanton continued. "That's why they've done well side by side. But Nimrod says the wolf'll become lazy. He's learnin' to prey on the settlers' livestock. Yer Sandy Hollow will come to know the wolf, little sister, but he won't be sent by the Devil." Stanton went back to stirring the kettle. "He'll be *invited*, little sister. By yer brethen."

The long-handled knife stabbed the kettle of water and came up with a length of boiled eel. The meat was pink and thick as a musket barrel. Ruth had eaten eel before and liked it. Stanton gave her a piece.

"This is from Nimrod," he said. "From the brook back there. He left the skin, too." The sharp knife pointed to the stones surrounding the fire pit, where a black eel skin lay. "When it dries, you can tie back yer hair. Nimrod says you should not walk about with yer hair in yer eyes. You must see clearly, now that yer a woman."

Ruth felt herself blush, the blood rising from her neck to warm her ears.

Stanton sat down in the grass with his portion of the eel. "I'll cut the skin into strips before I go."

Ruth looked up sharply. "*Go?* Will ye be going?"

"There's a party of trappers upstream. They'll be meetin' with the Indians to trade. I'm 'Mr. Many Tongues.' My service is needed."

"But—"

"Jes' rest here 'til I get back, little sister, then we'll figger out a way to get ye home. Yer Nimrod refuses to go to Cupheag. That's why he sent his smoke. He fears the English. He says a Red Man must not walk out of the woods with a White Woman who has seen the wolf."

Ruth blushed again.

"Nor should a White Man neither, for that matter." Stanton paused thoughtfully, turning the eel meat in his hands. He bit into the piece, holding it before him like an ear of corn. Then he continued, as if talking to himself. "The Indians have walked this land for years, cultivatin' no more soil than they needed. In the beginnin' they welcomed the White Man with hospitality. 'The land is forever,' Nimrod says. But now the White Man just takes the land. None of it were purchased, not a single square yard."

Baring his yellow teeth, Stanton tore away another chunk of eel meat. "There was a time," he went on, "when the Pequannocks and other tribes feared the Pequots more than they feared the English. But now the Pequots are gone and the English remain, spreadin' over the land like milkweed."

His jawbone clicked rhythmically as he chewed, his ragged sideburns riding up and down. A long silence settled over the clearing. Ruth could hear the brook behind her in the pines. It appeared that Stanton was finished speaking.

"Will ye tell me about the Pequot War?" Ruth asked finally. "I were younger then. Things were kept from me. I don't really know what happened."

Stanton cocked his head at an angle and studied Ruth. He drew in a deep breath that ended with a sigh. "The trouble goes back to 1614," he said, "when Captain John Smith left some men in charge of his ship. Those men took twenty-seven Indians prisoner and sold 'em as slaves. The Pequots never forgot that. It slumbered in their breasts."

The sun slipped behind a bank of high white clouds, putting the clearing in shadow. Stanton's voice seemed distant. "A great plague followed, so revenge were impossible. Then more and more Englishmen arrived and began to push westward. The Pequots were resolved to destroy 'em. They fired their houses, killed their cattle, and waited in ambush to shoot 'em as they went about their business. By 1637, they had killed thirty out of the two hundred settlers along the Connecticut River."

"We were at Windsor then," Ruth said. "I remember the massacre at Wethersfield. There were great fires. In the morning the sky was black with smoke."

"The Pequots were ruthless," Stanton said. "Most dreaded tribe in all New England. They forced the weaker tribes to fight with 'em. Sassacus—their sachem—was mean and tricky. I were trappin' to the north when the General Court put John Mason in charge. Men were levied out of Hartford, Wethersfield, Windsor—"

"Aye," Ruth set her eel meat abruptly in the grass. "I remember when my—"

"Out of Massachusetts Bay, too: Newberry, Dorchester, Salem, Charlestown. The settlers faced bein' wiped out. The Pequots swore to drive 'em right into the sea. Captain Mason sent for me to act as interpreter."

Stanton crossed his legs Indian style and stared at the ground between his knees, chewing and talking at the same time. "John Mason were a lucky fool," he said suddenly. "He didn't wait for the men from Massachusetts. He sailed up the Sound to the Pequot fort on the Mystic River—seventy-seven men to attack seven hundred warriors. They went in canoes, skiffs, anythin' that would float. He had some four hundred local Indians on his side, too, but they lagged behind. They were afraid to face the Pequots."

Stanton brushed aside some pine needles and, with his finger, drew a rough map in the dirt: the Sound, the Mystic river, the long Connecticut coastline across from Sewenhacky.

"When the little band passed the mouth of the river and kept on goin', the Pequots stood on the shore and laughed, thinkin' the White Men had gone on in fear. But Mason turned up the coast and marched inland. That night, as they camped close by the Pequot fort, they could hear the Red Men whoopin' it up around their fires." Stanton brushed away his map and drew a circle in the dirt. "The Pequot fort was a circular palisade enclosin' two acres of cleared land. Seventy wigwams were arranged in rows inside. There were two entrances on opposite sides of the fort, covered with thick brush." Stanton drew the entrances, then continued. "Dividin' his men, Mason attacked after midnight from each entrance. As they approached, a dog started barking within the palisade. 'Owanux!' the Pequots cried; Englishmen! That cry were the beginnin' of the end."

Stanton picked up his hat absentmindedly, the eagle feather standing erect. The leftover berries spilled into the grass. Ruth listened intently, lost in the story. Clouds still hid the sun.

"The men began to fire through the palisade," Stanton continued quickly. "Mason led the attack at one entrance, knocking aside the brush and branches. The Pequots were defenseless, taken completely by surprise. Wigwams were set afire, and the wind swept the flames across the fort. The savages fled into the smoke or tried to climb the palisade. Some charged and got the sword, others tried to shoot arrows but were no match for musket and shot. Within an hour, seven hundred were dead, the fort in ashes. Six managed to escape, but the local Indians—yer Niantics, Narragansetts, Mohegans—took care of 'em at a safe distance."

Stanton shook his bald head slowly, as if in judgment. "Mason were damn lucky. Had that dog barked any sooner, they would have been outnumbered ten to one."

The Indian interpreter paused, and Ruth thought his tale had ended. She drew her legs up and hugged her knees, but Stanton continued suddenly, in the same deliberate tone.

"There was a second fort with a few warriors left. Mason chased 'em clear up the coast, fightin' on the run. The Pequots were hampered by the slowness of their women and children. They crossed the Pootatuck and there was fightin' at Cupheag, right there at yer Sandy Hollow, little sister. Then, a few miles farther west, they were surrounded in a place called Saco Swamp. The Pequannocks were with 'em, women and children, too. Mason sent me in—he didn't want another massacre—and I treated with 'em. About two hundred came forth to be spared. And one of them, little sister, was yer Nimrod."

Ruth stared at the ground intently, the blades of grass blurring before her eyes. "What happened to the others?" she asked softly.

"Captured next mornin' as they tried to flee the swamp. About a hundred and eighty, the last of the Pequots. Mason ordered 'em dispersed among the other tribes as slaves. They were forbidden to be called Pequot any longer. Uncas, sachem of the Mohegans, saw it done. He hated 'em so."

Stanton looked at Ruth. His voice grew restless, louder now, summing up. "It were amazin'. In such a hostile territory, and so greatly outnumbered, with only Indians for scouts. There were more than a share of miracles, little sister. Take John Dier and Thomas Stiles: both were shot in the neck, right in the knot of their handkerchiefs, and so received no hurt. Lieutenant Bull took an arrow in a piece of hard cheese, and was spared."

Stanton laughed in disbelief. "In the whole campaign, Captain Mason lost only two men, and he needn't have lost those if he had waited. There was Jonathan Walker and Jonas P—"

"Paine," Ruth said quietly. "Jonas Paine. That were my Papa."

7.

Discussions in Darkness

THE moon reflected brilliantly in the river outside the Meeting House. The crickets and katydids were unusually noisy. Inside, a lone candle flickered on the desk beside the pulpit. Shadows of the men moved dimly on the wall.

"No doubt she's a hostage to the Red Man!" Captain Mason asserted. He sat in the middle of the front bench, with Sergeant Nichols and Moses Wheeler on either side. Nicolas Knell, as narrow as the lone candle, stood off to the left. The others, including young John Blakeman, filled the benches behind. "Give an Indian an inch and he'll take an ell!"

Seated at the desk, Reverend Blakeman toyed with the hourglass. He had taken its white sand from the beach at Ipswich before sailing from England. Now it flowed back and forth as if with his thoughts as he stared at the bloodstained shells in front of him.

He looked up at Captain Mason, then looked away.

"Tell us again, son. Where did'st thou find these?"

Young John Blakeman stood quickly. "At the shore, father, in the sand at the bluffs, at the base of a mountain of shells!"

"Indian mound!" Captain Mason declared. "A sacred feast site. There be several like it 'twixt here and Manhattas, and several more across the Sound on Sewenhacky. We discovered them while chasing the Pequots."

The men rumbled, whispering among themselves.

Reverend Blakeman looked to Moses Wheeler, and the large

man nodded. Nicolas Knell nodded too, tugging on his long white beard.

"We know of the mound," the Reverend said.

"You have seen it, father?" Young John Blakeman was still standing, his blue eyes glinting excitedly in the candlelight.

"Moses found it while scouting the Old Field. Goodman Knell divined its purpose. It were kept quiet. It would alarm the women and children to know that our Sandy Hollow—our Stratford—were settled on ground sacred to the Heathen."

Young John Blakeman swallowed hard, unable to contain his surprise.

"I'll go to the Pequannocks first thing in the morning," Captain Mason said. "They'll remember me. I could have massacred them all and left their bones in Saco Swamp! They'll remember me. I'll learn what's afoot." He turned to his right. "What's the arsenal?"

Sergeant Nichols jumped from the bench, his hand on the heel of his sword. "Three hundred weight of lead, one hundred fathom of match, and one barrel of powder, sir! There be six corselets, too, with serviceable pikes!"

"Francis!" the Reverend shouted. "Possess thy soul in patience! I am sure the General Court meant thy train-band as a safeguard only. The Pequot War ended three years ago. Be that not correct, Captain Mason?"

Sergeant Nichols sat down, and young John Blakeman melted into his seat under the Reverend's stare. "Mr. Mason?"

The Captain was silent.

"Good God Gravy, man!" Moses Wheeler bellowed. "Answer the minister!"

Captain Mason's chin sunk to his chest. "Aye, sir. The war be over."

"Then let us not stir up another!" Reverend Blakeman's bushy eyebrows shot up and down, his face and beard strangely lighted behind the candle. "Now tell us, please, of these Pequannocks."

Captain Mason cleared his throat and stood up, towering as tall and broad as the elevated pulpit. "They be your neighbors, sir. To the west. Several hundred or more, by Saco Swamp. 'Pequannock' means 'cleared field.' They carved several acres right out of the middle of the forest with space for corn and space to live. Their wigwams are leafy and shaped like bread-loaves. The men hunt inland and fish in the Sound."

"And have we reason to fear them, Captain?" Reverend Blakeman set the hourglass aside, all the sand in the bottom bulb.

"No reason, sir, until now. For the first time in three years they neglect their tribute to the General Court. And suddenly thy Ruth disappears. I know the Indians, sir. Give an inch and they'll take—"

"An ell."

"Exactly!"

Silence fell over the Meeting House, as deep as the darkness outside. Reverend Blakeman stared intently at the shells on the desk, his thoughts revolving as slowly as the grindstone at the tidal mill. "And what of Ruth's name in the sand? What of the blood?"

No one answered. The candle flickered and diminished, then flared a bright yellow.

"A sign, sir," Captain Mason said finally. "A warning."

"But they know not her name, and Ruth speaks only English. Do these Pequannocks speak English?"

"Not a syllable."

The candle flame diminished, then leaped again.

"And be there other tribes?"

"Paugassetts to the north, Waramaugs to the east. Fewer in number, and so far silent."

"And pay they their tribute?"

"Aye, sir, but less than the Pequannocks. They killed no English in the Pequot War."

Reverend Blakeman folded his hands on the desk. "Then there be no grievances."

"What grievance can the Red Man have, sir? They were spared their lives. We brought them news of Christ."

Extending his forefinger, Reverend Blakeman slowly rearranged the shells in front of him, sliding them about until they spelled out R-U-T-H. Then he inverted the hourglass, sand spilling freely into the bottom bulb. "I counsel patience," he said firmly. "And prayer."

While the men held their conference at the Meeting House, Anna Paine paced the earthen floor of her cabin. Her broad fists, thrust deep into the wrinkled pocket of her apron, had squeezed John Blakeman's green pine cone again and again.

As in the Meeting House, a lone candle lit the room, from a clay holder that rested on an empty nail keg.

"Stratford!" the widow mumbled. "Call it what ye will—my Ruth be gone!" Her gray hair, unpinned and unkempt, hung straight to her wide shoulders. Her face was ashen, her short stub of a nose red from wiping.

A loaded musket—Jonas Paine's own, retrieved from the Pequot fort the morning after the massacre—rested on a crude pine table along the far wall, within reach of Ruth's empty pallet. The widow's bed, a narrow wooden frame with a thin straw mattress, lay unmade in the corner.

A large black kettle hung in the stone fireplace, as empty as her heart. The log mantel held an earthenware jug, several wooden plates, and two pewter spoons.

Naked beams ran parallel overhead. A square, dark opening in the ceiling led to a shallow loft used for storage. In the loft was an old trunk with woolen cloaks for winter, and wooden crates with the personal effects of Jonas Paine.

Anna Paine stared at Ruth's empty pallet. "What ails thee, Ruth, that ye'd run off on the Sabbath to write thy name in bloody shells? Would that ye were only hidin' aloft and playin' some child's game! Lord help us!"

Holding her face in her rough hands, she sobbed loudly, drowning out the light rap at the door.

In a moment the rapping came again, and the widow heard it. Had the Lord returned Ruth in answer to her prayer? If it were so—if it were only so—she would never again allow the girl to miss the Sabbath. Nor herself, for that matter. She would try again to learn to read, so she could study the word of God. And certainly she would have Ruth learn to read the Good Book! Aye, she would. She promised!

The knocking came again, more insistent, and Anna Paine trudged to the door. "Ruth?" she cried. "Ruth!"

A tall, dark figure stood on the stone step. It was Goody Blakeman, the Reverend's wife, with Goody Thomson frowning over her shoulder.

Neither woman had visited the cabin before. In the northwest corner of the palisade, it was easy to avoid, especially when one was uncertain as to the rumors that flew in its direction.

Goody Thomson's mouth dropped open as she stared past Anna Paine into the dim, stark interior. "We come," she said at last, "to—"

"—to offer comfort," the Reverend's wife finished. "God is our refuge and our strength, our greatest help in trouble."

Anna Paine closed the door halfway. "If ye wish to help, then go find my daughter."

"The men have tried, Anna Paine, and will try yet again tomorrow."

The widow scowled. "Then nothing's to be done."

Goody Blakeman put her foot within the door. "Thy daught—thy Ruth—may be gone, Anna Paine, but keep in mind: 'Absent in body, but present in spirit.' "

"First Corinthians," Goody Thomson said. "Chapter 5, Verse 3."

Goody Blakeman smiled. "Put your trust in the Lord."

Anna Paine closed the door even farther, pushing it against Jane Blakeman's foot. She glared at the Reverend's wife. "What? Will ye do thy husband's work?"

Goody Blakeman withdrew her foot indignantly. " 'A virtuous woman is a crown to her husband.' "

"Proverbs!" Goody Thomson said. "Chapter 12, Verse 4."

The widow laughed. "And hast thou brought a parrot to the New World?"

The Reverend's wife stuck her hands on her hips. Her nostrils flared. "Now listen to me, Anna Paine. We come for thy comfort, not thy insults! Thy d—thy Ruth be missing."

Goody Thomson raised a finger. "The Word of God is a sword, Anna Paine!"

"Aye, and thou take'st it for a fire poke!"

The heavy log door slammed shut. The yellow candle flame bent in the breeze.

Outside, the women hurried away.

" 'There be things that are never satisfied,' " Goody Blakeman huffed. " 'The grave and the barren womb!' "

"Aye," Goody Thomson assented. "Proverbs: Chapter 30, Verse 16."

8.

Signs and Symbols

THOMAS STANTON was gone a week, longer than he expected. A second party of traders—Dutchmen trapping east from Hudson's River—had crossed his path and requested to do business with the Indians. In spite of the delay, he agreed to help them, knowing that Ruth was safe downstream.

At first, Ruth waited patiently, content with his promise to return. He had left his long bone-handled knife with her, plus the black kettle and a supply of driftwood to fuel the fire. He had shown her how to gather wild carrots and turnips, which she collected daily to boil into soup. He had explained how to tell the difference between the mushrooms she could eat and those that were certain to be disagreeable. She picked blackberries and raspberries, too.

Every afternoon, following the grassy path from the clearing to the shore of the Pootatuck, Ruth hung her drab smock on the branch of a birch and swam in the sparkling water. Floating on her back, she would drift long distances with the current, then roll over to dog-paddle back upstream. Schools of minnows flashed in the shallows, fleeing when she tried to cup them in her hands. From among the overhanging pines, bluejays screamed at one another for no apparent reason. And once Ruth thought she saw a tern knifing its way high above the river, miles from its home along the Sound.

The sleek bird reminded her of the shell heap. How to make

sense of the strange events of the past week? Would she ever see Sandy Hollow again? Where was Stanton? Why hadn't he returned?

Before long, Ruth found that the dark blood between her thighs was lessening. Then it was gone altogether, much to her relief. She washed her smock at the river's edge, pounding it with large round stones as she had learned from Widow Paine. But the brown bloodstains remained.

The smock was threadbare, tattered, and slit along the seams. Try as she might, Ruth could not tie it again into a breechclout the way Nimrod had. So she wore the smock as it was, letting it hang in wide strips from the waist. What would John Blakeman think of such an outfit? she wondered.

At night, when the deep blackness settled over the clearing and the damp cold crept in, she pulled the smock tightly around her legs, huddling by the fire for warmth. The rust-red pelt was as big as a blanket and looked so inviting, but its pine stakes had been driven deep into the earth and she was not strong enough to remove them.

She slept soundly the first few nights, still recovering from her wound, but on the following nights she began to wake suddenly, numbed by a chill, the fire in the pit all but out. She lacked the practice to make the gathered brush and driftwood burn slowly. She slept less and less, dreading the purple haze that signaled the coming dusk.

She wished that Thomas Stanton would return.

Then, on the fifth or sixth night—the days had blurred beyond an accurate accounting—she arranged the sticks of driftwood on the firebed as best she could and fell asleep, exhausted, almost at once.

As if under a spell, she began to dream—dream of large dark eyes that watched her from the woods; steady eyes, deliberate and patient. She dreamed of a crackling bonfire, its yellow flames leaping high, spreading snug warmth and contentment.

She dreamed she was carried by the Pootatuck, her body cupped in the water as she had cupped her hands to hold the minnows.

It was a long sleep, deep and needed, and not once did she stir in the night. In the morning when she woke she found the sun high in the sky and the rust-red wolf pelt wrapped around her.

Yet she was alone in the clearing!

Then she saw on the blackened stones that surrounded the fire pit several small piles of gray ash, standing like anthills, neatly deposited from the stone bowl of a Red Man's pipe.

Nimrod! Come and gone in the night.

Returning to his cabin from the meeting with Captain Mason, Sergeant Nichols had found his wife in bed, delirious with fever. He had boiled water for sassafras tea, but Mary Nichols knocked the wooden cup from his hand. Throughout the night he sought to comfort her, mopping her brow, smoothing her hair, but by morning she lay cold in his arms.

The death of Mary Nichols shocked the settlers of Stratford—the first among them since their departure from England. Captain Mason missed the news, sailing before dawn from the mouth of the Pootatuck and tacking west up the Sound toward the Pequannocks.

The search for Ruth was abruptly suspended.

Late that afternoon, Mary Nichols was buried in a small grave to the north of the Meeting House, on a grassy knoll along the riverbank. The site, chosen quickly and at random by Reverend Blakeman, was to become the settlement's permanent graveyard.

"She were ill for England," Sergeant Nichols said, as the small band stood in a circle about the grave. "The very sea journey left her ill. It broke her spirit. Her strength were gone and she never recovered."

"Not all are fit and able to do the Lord's work," Reverend

Blakeman said in a louder voice. Dressed in black, he cut a somber figure at the foot of the grave. "May she rest in peace. On the heels of our anniversary Sabbath, the Lord hath sent us a reminder of our frailty."

Anna Paine mumbled to herself, thinking only of Ruth. Her eyes were puffed and bleary, her hands clasped within the pocket of her apron.

Moses Wheeler tossed a spadeful of red earth over the pine casket he had hastily constructed. He had set to work on the narrow box even before Reverend Blakeman had arrived at his home-lot in request of his services. He had excavated the grave, too, in a matter of minutes.

Nicolas Knell nodded at the Reverend and left the grave site quietly, tugging on his long white beard. It was a clear day, cooler than usual, high white clouds streaming in from the north.

"Grief is sufficient unto the day thereof," the Reverend said to the others. "Let us not dwell within it."

Jane Blakeman turned for the Meeting House where Sexton Peake was keeping the children. She was angry with herself. "To think," she said over her shoulder to Goody Thomson, "that we wasted our good time at the cabin of one whose name I shan't mention, when there was another among us so in need of succor! The poor dear! The Lord forgive us in our blindness!"

Goody Thomson said nothing. It was all she could do to keep up.

"Let us resume the search for Ruth within the hour!" Reverend Blakeman ordered. "Same parties as were yesterday named!"

The men dispersed. The women collected their children and returned to the home-lots, talking in terse tones amongst themselves. Mary Nichols dead! Had she offended the Lord? Sergeant Nichols had been the last to see Ruth, and now Mary Nichols dead!

The search for Ruth continued without success. Stratford's crops were neglected. The men ranged farther and farther from the protection of the palisade into the forests to the north and west, only to return dejectedly each evening.

At the end of the week, Captain Mason returned, anchoring his ship at midstream. He was irritated. Having visited the Pequannocks and surveyed the western bounds of Stratford, he had found no sign of Ruth.

"Queriheag, sachem of the Pequannocks, was insulted! They know nothing of the girl. They send no wampum because of poor hunting. They claim the white settlers and trappers disturb the patterns of wild game."

The Captain stood in his dinghy at the wharf, shouting through cupped hands to Reverend Blakeman on the riverbank, the little boat rocking unsteadily beneath him. "While I was there, one of their hunters, called Nimrod, returned from a powwow with the Paugassetts and Waramaugs. They also claim poor hunting!"

"We appreciate thine efforts, sir!" Reverend Blakeman called back.

"I wish I could aid thee further, but we are overdue at the General Court. If Ruth be not found—!"

"We will find her, Captain!"

Captain Mason's large brown eyes blazed fiercely. "If a thing be proper and possible to man, thou art the man to do it!"

"With the Lord's help!"

"The Lord will provide!"

Small, black waves slapped the wharf, filling the short silence that followed. Then Captain Mason saluted, pointed to his ship, and the lad seated behind him put his back to the oars.

The scrawny, reddish-brown cow stared stupidly into the trees at the edge of the pasture. It had wandered, slowly, away from the rest of the herd, stepping around the stumps that had not been cleared from the New Field.

Flies buzzed its wide ears, which stuck straight out like flags, waving absently at the insects.

The animal turned its head and stared back toward the palisade. The rest of the herd grazed quietly, foraging among the weeds, their pale udders heavy with milk. Tails swished above their rumps, jerking upwards, then flopping down, swatting at the ever-present flies. Each tail was at least three feet long, like a braided rope, ending in a brush of coarse hair.

The cow lowered its head to graze. Suddenly, there was a swift movement at its tail. The flies thickened, buzzing loudly, biting its flanks. Looking behind, the cow saw nothing. Its tail had become a stub, twitching back and forth.

The cow began to run, lumbering across the pasture in a swarm of flies. Rejoining the herd, it wedged itself between two others, relieved by the sweep of their tails.

The flies dispersed. The cows grazed undisturbed.

At sunset, when young John Blakeman was sent to gather the herd, the cow was greeted with shouts of surprise. The shouting continued as men came running, returning from the search for Ruth.

"What, ho!" Sergeant Nichols yelled from the Watchhouse. He hurried down the ladder and out the gate, toward the growing crowd hastening the cows within the palisade.

"Good God Gravy!" Moses Wheeler roared. "Lookee there! Its tail's been bobbed!"

"Clean as a whistle," the Reverend said.

Nicholas Knell put both hands to his long white beard, as if fearing it should meet the same fate. "Tomahawk," was all he said.

Sergeant Nichols arrived, out of breath. "What, ho!"

The surrounded cow looked at the men innocently. Six inches from its rump the once long tail ended abruptly in a nub of bristles.

"So this be Queriheag's answer!" the Sergeant said.

"And Captain Mason just departed! Good God Gravy!"

Reverend Blakeman stared out the gate across the empty pasture into the woods beyond. Already the trees were a mass of black in the falling twilight. "Set torches along the palisade!" he cried. "Prepare for ambush! Sexton Peake, sound thy bell! The heathen devils be at home in the black of night like the Prince of Darkness himself! In God's truth, they be in league!"

Young John Blakeman's mouth fell open. Bolting from the crowd, he hurried away to find his mother and report the news. Sergeant Nichols turned and ran for the arsenal.

Reverend Blakeman shouted orders. "All women and children to the Meeting House! Bring provisions for the night! Then report to Sergeant Nichols at the Watchhouse!"

The men dispersed, leaving the herd in a circle within the gate. Blinking contentedly among the others, the cow lowered its head to the grass, its short tail conducting an unheard tune.

Within minutes the general alarm sounded, Sexton Peake pulling again and again on the thick rope of the bell tower.

No trees stood within fifty yards of the palisade, lest the Red Man have an aid in attack. The home-lots lay north to south in two long lanes, facing inward to form a broad avenue.

Torches soon appeared, dark figures huddled beneath, moving from the home-lots across the settlement. All candles had been extinguished within the cabins. The shouting had stopped. The processions of women and children moved quietly, escorted by men in arms.

The Blakeman family was the first to reach the Meeting House, their home-lot adjacent to the grounds. "Go fetch the Widow Paine from her corner cabin," the Reverend instructed his eldest son. He lit the candle on the desk beside the pulpit and inverted the brassbound hourglass.

Settling her children into their places, Jane Blakeman looked up sharply, giving her husband a worried glance. She fought a lump in her throat as her son ran off.

The families filed in. Coarse blankets were piled on the benches, bowls of apples and jugs of water were passed around.

Jane Blakeman stood in the doorway, quietly greeting everyone who entered, watching for her son, who did not return.

Minutes later, Reverend Blakeman found young John at the arsenal, where he had gone after warning Widow Paine. Jonas Paine's musket was in his grasp. John avoided his father's eyes, and his father said nothing.

Standing beneath the Watchhouse, in the short doorway to the stockade, Sergeant Nichols issued powder and shot. "Spread thyselves along the palisade," he cried. "Afix thy torch and watch the fields for moving shadows!"

Dark clouds hid the moon. The cows, unattended, wandered about the home-lots, disturbing chickens at their roost.

Nicolas Knell climbed to the lookout to join Reverend Blakeman. "The moon be no help tonight, sir," he said. "The torches show only our own positions. Have the women make us more, to be set in a ring, out there!" Removing his hand from his beard momentarily, Nicolas Knell pointed into the darkness of the New Field.

Reverend Blakeman nodded. "I'll see it done."

Sexton Peake, arriving to report all in order at the Meeting House, was immediately dispatched to set the women to work.

Within an hour the job was completed. Sheaves of straw lay bound to thick sticks.

Slipping into the night from the northern gate, Moses Wheeler and Sergeant Nichols crossed the pasture to set the unlit torches in place. Muskets loaded, the men behind them stared into the blackness for signs of ambush.

When all torches were set out, Sergeant Nichols turned quietly to Moses Wheeler. "Return, now, to the palisade and I'll set them aflame!"

"Good God Gravy! I'll stand and guard thee!"

"Nay, the job need but one. With Pequannocks about we be sitting chickens!"

The two men huddled in the far corner of the New Field, arguing within yards of the woods.

"That be an *order*, sir, from the Sergeant of thy train-band, an order form the General Court!" The Sergeant's voice rose above a whisper.

"Good God Gravy!"

"Do as I say, man!"

"Aye, and ye'll join thy Mary!"

Lunging forward, Sergeant Nichols grabbed the big man's thick wrist, wrestling with him briefly until he recognized the other was too powerful. He released his grip and the scuffling stopped.

"If ye won't take an order, Mr. Wheeler, then do it for *Stratford's* sake! One man lost be better than two!"

Moses Wheeler crouched in the darkness for a long moment, staring back at the lights along the palisade. Sandy Hollow was not yet Stratford to him. Sergeant Nichols were either a patriot or a fool.

Finally, giving a mock salute, he crept away. By the time he had made his way back across the field, a ring of torches blazed at the edge of the distant woods.

9.

The Return

SERGEANT Nichols did not retreat to the palisade. "I should have stayed with him!" Moses Wheeler declared.

"The Sergeant hath turned his grief into considerable bravery."

"Or recklessness, Reverend." Nicolas Knell studied the outlying torches, their leaping red flames shooting wild shadows against the far wall of trees. "It be Halloween for sure."

"Good God Gravy, I should have stayed!"

"The woods are silent. No sounds. Not a one."

"Aye, but the Red Man can stand right behind thee unheard 'til his tomahawk runs with blood from thy scalp." Nicolas Knell stroked his beard with both hands, holding more white hair than covered his head.

"We can only wait and be ready," Reverend Blakeman said. "Let us keep the Sergeant's absence to ourselves."

At the Meeting House, Jane Blakeman inverted the hourglass for the third time. The children slept together, huddled among blankets in the corner, and Sexton Peake, exhausted from running back and forth, lay stretched out on the first bench, snoring fitfully.

"One more hour," Goody Thomson moaned, "and it be the Sabbath again, one week since Ruth . . ." She looked to the door and her voice trailed off. Widow Paine claimed the rear bench in a wide-eyed trance, arms folded stiffly across her broad chest, a carving knife balanced on her knees.

"Hush, dear," said Jane Blakeman mechanically. She sat at the desk beside the pulpit, staring at the white sands of Ipswich

73

as they fell freely into the bottom bulb of the hourglass. The lone candle had but an inch remaining.

As the dark night lengthened, the men fixed themselves in their positions along the palisade. In the New Field, the torches burned low. Gradually the surrounding blackness yielded to purple, then lightened to gray. Roosters stirred and crowed within the home-lots. Several cows were standing on the parade ground. John Blakeman pulled his father's frock coat about his ears, asleep behind a barrel of powder in the arsenal.

The men behind the muskets soon found themselves wrapped in a rolling white fog. Fear increased lest the painted Red Man emerge whooping from the ghostly soup.

Finally, Sexton Peake arrived from the Meeting House, carrying a basket of apples and bread. Feeling his way along the palisade, he supplied each sentry, then climbed the ladder to the Watchhouse, his footsteps waking John Blakeman below.

Embarrassed, the Reverend's son grabbed his musket and hurried to join the others.

In the Watchhouse tower, Moses Wheeler turned to greet the Sexton.

"Movement!" Reverend Blakeman shouted suddenly. "*There!*" He pointed to his right, to where the woods beyond the New Field met the river.

Goodman Peake dropped his basket, the remaining apples rolling across the platform. The word leaped along the palisade. *Movement!* All eyes strained into the grainy mist. To the north, by the river, the steaming ground merged with the smoky air.

The movement came again, shadowy figures between layers of fog. Muskets swayed, trigger fingers ready.

"Wait 'til they be in range!" the Reverend ordered. "Wait!"

East of the Pootatuck, the sun hit the horizon, sending forth a wide plane of light.

"What, ho!"

Through a brightening cloud of fog came Sergeant Nichols, leading Ruth by the hand. "What, ho!" he cried again. "I have the girl!"

The northern gate of the palisade flew open and the men broke into the field, powder horns bobbing at their backs. Sexton Peake ran for the Meeting House. "Found!" he yelled. "Safe and sound!"

Bright morning sunlight washed across the settlement, the grass suddenly aglitter with dew.

Fifty yards from the palisade, the crowd of men stopped short, halted by the spectacle before them. Ruth came out of the fog wrapped in a rust-red wolf pelt. Her frizzy red hair, tied back with eel skin, was decked with white daisies and black-eyed Susans. She seemed clean and fresh beside the dusty buckskins of the puzzled Sergeant.

No one spoke. John Blakeman blinked in disbelief, holding Jonas Paine's musket as if to take aim. The Reverend pushed the barrel toward the earth and stepped forward.

A wide smile crossed Sergeant Nichol's dirty face. "I spent the night in a stump pit," he said finally, "an advanced guard against possible attack, hearing nothing until a moment ago, and then—*this!*" He dropped Ruth's hand and stood back as if to study her. "I thought it were the spirit of my Mary!"

Ruth, who had been staring shyly at her bare feet in the grass, looked up for the first time. "*Spirit?*"

"Our Mary Nichols departed this world," the Reverend informed, "soon after you disappeared."

Sergeant Nichols bit his lip. "Aye, Ruth. From a fever. It were sudden."

Ruth's eyes glistened like the dew. She put her head to the Sergeant's dusty shoulder. "Mary Nichols were ever a friend," she said quietly. She looked around at the stunned faces of the men. Somehow her words seemed a warning.

Without his frock coat, the Reverend rubbed his arms for warmth. The men were waiting for him to speak, but he seemed at a loss for words. "Child," he said at last, "where hast thou been these seven days?"

Ruth stammered, "I—lost my way."

"We found thy name writ in shells at the bluffs."

"I—wandered from the shell mound. I became lost in the woods."

Ruth turned and looked behind her, to the misty forest from which she had emerged. In the broad shafts of sunlight, the green leaves shone.

Reverend Blakeman looked away, shaking his head. Nicolas Knell tugged his beard. The small band of men still kept their distance.

"And the wolf pelt, child? Whence? How?"

"I wandered in the woods looking for the Sound, until I found myself at the river—in a clearing, a hunter's camp. The skin were staked to the ground."

Moses Wheeler scratched his head. "Good God Gravy! Who would go through the trouble to brain-cure a pelt, then up and abandon it?"

All eyes turned to Ruth, but she was silent.

"The Red Man claims poor hunting," Nicolas Knell reminded. "That were Captain Mason's report. Perhaps . . . perhaps a trapper would leave his camp, ranging wide."

Reverend Blakeman studied Ruth.

"And the band about thy head?"

"Eel skin—found on stones about the fire pit."

The Reverend's bushy eyebrows danced up and down, his brow furrowing as he considered the sight before him. "There were blood on the shells, child."

"I—" Again Ruth looked behind her to the forest, as if she might suddenly bolt away. "The shells were sharp," she said bluntly. "I cut myself."

Reverend Blakeman stepped forward. "Show us thy wound."

Ruth extended a clenched fist, slowly opening her fingers, her small palm to the sky. A thin line of dried blood ran across the base of her thumb. Digging for sassafras roots as she waited for Thomas Stanton, she had sliced herself on his bone-handled knife.

Reverend Blakeman looked to Nicolas Knell, and the old man nodded, tugging his beard.

"Full circle," the Reverend muttered to himself. "South to the bluffs, west along the Sound, north and east to the river, then south again home." His voice grew louder. "She hath come full circle." He paused, as if to let the significance of his words sink in.

Behind him the men waited anxiously. Nicolas Knell nodded again.

"And what be a circle," the Reverend continued, "but a symbol of perfection, the very pattern of the planets and the stars, the very design of the heavens? Our Ruth hath wandered full circle and come safely home. It be a miracle! It be God's will!"

A general shout rose from the small band into the morning sunlight. The fog was lifting, drifting in small patches along the river. Several reddish-brown cows had wandered from the northern gate.

Nicolas Knell pointed a bony finger at the small herd, and the Reverend suddenly remembered. "To the palisade!" he warned, "lest the Pequannocks be watching!"

The men grew serious, their sudden joy giving way to old fears. The torches stood forlornly in the stump pits, a ring of charred stakes at the perimeter of the woods.

Sergeant Nichols hugged Ruth to his side. "But there were no sign of the Pequannocks the entire night, sir. I lay awake and heard nothing."

Ruth looked up from beneath the Sergeant's arm. "*Pequannocks?*"

Young John Blakeman could contain himself no longer. Stepping out from behind his father he blurted, "One of the cows lost a tail to a tomahawk! I discovered it myself! The Pequannocks wait to attack!"

Ruth stared at the Reverend's son queerly, the father's frock coat too large for his skinny limbs. She recognized the weapon in his grasp.

The men looked to her anxiously, as if to a prophet.

"Tomahawk?" she said quietly. "It were probably a wolf."

10.

The Eyes in the Woods

WIDOW Paine took Ruth into her broad, open arms and returned with her immediately to their home-lot. Shutting the thick cabin door behind them, she asked no questions. She had lost a husband, but her daughter had returned. She would not face the days ahead alone. A smile flickered across her face again and again as she prepared their morning porridge.

The settlers left the pair alone for their reunion. "Prepare for the Sabbath!" Reverend Blakeman instructed. "A special day of thanksgiving! The Lord hath seen fit to return our Ruth—a miracle! She hath come full circle!"

The Pequannocks were momentarily forgotten as the weary men gathered their families and returned to their home-lots to make ready for a long day of worship.

Later in the morning, addressing his congregation at the Meeting House, Reverend Blakeman outdid himself. He constructed his sermon around Ruth's experience. The Lord loved Ruth Paine, he said. She was a child of the New World and had been blessed with a special strength. She had walked into the forest and returned unscathed. Was it not a sign from Heaven? A sign that the children of the New World, the future generations of Stratford, would thrive?

The shell gash on Ruth's thumb was a warning, the Reverend said, a symbol of the physical hardships harbored by the New World. It was a reminder that the New World was inhabited by heathens. It was the heathen who had constructed the huge shell mound at the bluffs. But with the Lord at one's side, one could walk away from such a mound. Such a small wound as Ruth had suffered, symbolic of temptation, would readily heal.

Ruth's eyes glistened. She sat in her accustomed seat at the rear of the Meeting House, staring at the dirt floor, ignoring the quick glances sent in her direction. She wore a plain brown frock, her only remaining summer garment. The wolf pelt lay at home across her pallet. Her tattered smock had been burned by Widow Paine, as if to put the events of the week behind them forever.

Ruth's mind wandered to Thomas Stanton. He had returned, full of apologies, to row her in his little skiff through the moonless darkness, down the Pootatuck to Sandy Hollow. Could it have been only yesterday?

Young John Blakeman fidgeted on his bench. It was impossible to concentrate on his father's words. Ruth seemed so much older, no longer such a flighty little girl.

After the service, the settlers chattered on the riverbank, shaking the Reverend's hand, breathing easily. The day that had begun in fear of attack had turned into a day of routine worship. How beautiful the summer weather! How soon the harvest!

Nicolas Knell motioned Moses Wheeler aside as the big man came out of the Meeting House. "Better the Pequannocks," he whispered, "than the *wolf*."

"Aye, the Pequannocks be once overcome already, but the wolf—"

Moses Wheeler smiled quickly at the approaching Jane Blakeman. The receiving line had ended, the settlers heading to their home-lots for the midday meal. "Good day, sister! Our weeks of trials be ended!"

Jane Blakeman stepped aside, shading the sun from her face with a tug on her cap. "Nay, brother, our trials be just started when we wear flowers and the skins of animals! Women should 'adorn themselves in modest apparel, with shamefacedness and sobriety; not with broided hair, or gold, or pearls—' "

"—'but with good works,' " Goody Thomson finished, " 'which becometh women professing godliness.' First Timothy; Chapter 2, Verses 9 and 10."

In the clearing by the stocks and whipping post Sergeant Nichols hailed young John Blakeman, the first recruit for his trainband. Ruth and Anna Paine were beyond him, already halfway to their home-lot.

September came. The men worked long hours in the Old Field, harvesting corn and plowing the golden stubble under. Each evening, within the palisade, the train-band drilled on the parade grounds until dark.

Widow Paine kept mostly to her cabin, boiling animal fat in the large kettle in the fireplace, preparing tallow against the long nights of the coming winter. She spoke to no one—spoke only to Ruth when she had to—and was contented with her busy, homely task. She dipped candles as if in a dream.

Autumn colors blazed in the distant woods. Twice a day Ruth carried water to the men in the fields, the wooden buckets dangling from her shoulder yoke. She was no longer confined to the palisade. As if her strange journey had earned her the privilege, she now came and went at will.

So the shell mound was sacred to the Red Man! Isn't that what Reverend Blakeman had said? What other evidence of the Red Man might be nearby? Ruth wondered. She decided to explore the settlement for further signs.

In a ledge at the perimeter of the New Field she found, sunk in bedrock, a smooth hole that was two feet wide and several inches deep. Not far away she unearthed a stone pestle. Here, she imagined, the Red Man had ground his corn.

On the bank of the Pootatuck she found, in another rock hidden by brush, an upright hollow—perhaps the Red Man's natural fireplace. Kneeling before it, she imagined a kettle suspended above the flames. Here the Red Man had stewed his meat.

A week later, digging in the loose dirt by the well at the gate, she uncovered a host of arrowheads, buried among chips and flakes of small hard stone. The well, a natural fresh-water spring, had been used by the Red Man; here he had fashioned his arrows.

Often, just at dusk, when the men left their work behind them in the fields and turned for the smoking chimneys of the home-lots, Ruth lingered among the farthest furrows, staring into the darkening woods. More than once she found her stare returned. A pair of watchful eyes would materialize in the purple shadows of the foliage and then disappear a long moment later. Ruth was never afraid. The eyes were steady and intense, yet comforting, always vanishing at the very moment that she was certain they were there. She was to see them again and again in the years to come.

And whenever she could, Ruth would slip away from the men in the Old Field and disappear in the tall grass along the bluffs. Sliding to the beach with her frock tucked beneath her, she would hike all the way to the shell heap. One morning, as she knelt beside the mound, she looked up to find John Blakeman standing above her. Jonas Paine's musket was slung across his arm. Picking up a short stick of driftwood, she began to write her name in the sand.

"Why do ye ignore me?" the Reverend's son asked.

"Why do ye carry my Papa's weapon?"

"It were given me by Widow Paine."

"She were distracted, unfit to reason."

"I'm a member of the train-band now. It is my duty to protect thee."

Ruth hesitated. "Did I need thy protection while away in the forest?"

Young John Blakeman shifted his eyes up the Sound, to

where the distant woods met the shore. Ruth had wandered there alone, unharmed. The very thought raised a lump in his throat.

"I—I want to be thy friend." His blue eyes blazed. "I care not what the others say."

Ruth drew the stick through the sand slowly, completing her handiwork: R-U-T-H. Then she turned abruptly, squinting into the autumn sunlight. John Blakeman seemed taller than ever, the cuffs of his linsey-woolsey shirt almost to his elbows.

"And what *do* the others say, Master Blakeman?"

"That thou'rt not so much a miracle as a mystery." His blond locks lifted in the off-shore breeze.

Ruth laughed.

"That ye conspired with Sergeant Nichols, the last to see thee, the first to find thee. Oh, Ruth, why did ye go to the woods?"

Ruth stared at her name in the sand, her tongue curling to the tip of her nose. Then she tossed the stick aside and looked up sharply. "If it be any of your business, Master Blakeman, I went to the woods to become a *woman*. Take *that* for a pine cone and smoke it!"

Kee-urr! Kee-urr!

High above the Sound, the terns wheeled and dove. The day had suddenly turned chilly. Slate skies checked the gleam of the shells. John Blakeman stared at Ruth, then pivoted smartly and walked away.

A feather, as sleek and light as the wing that had lost it, drifted downward out of the sky, skirting left, then right. It came to rest across the stick with which Ruth had drawn her name. Ruth laughed. The feather had crossed the stick to form a *T*, and the letters in the sand now read T-R-U-T-H.

Alone on the beach, Ruth sounded them out.

Kee-urr! Kee-urr!

A gust of wind blew the feather away.

PART II
Stratford, 1650

11.

Mr. Bassett

STRATFORD had changed considerably in its first ten years, and sometimes Ruth felt she was the only one who noticed. The others seemed too busy, lost in the daily routine of labor and household chores.

The roots and stumps that had been woven into crude fences around the New Field were gradually replaced by logs and boards. Grassy footpaths between the home-lots were worn to dirt lanes, then widened into muddy avenues. Many of the log cabins were replaced by one-story frame dwellings, several others by dwellings of stone.

Only the Paines' cabin remained untouched. The widow allowed no one to come near it, not even to replace with precious glass the oiled cloth that served as windows.

Moses Wheeler, applying to the General Court in Hartford, had been granted the right to keep a ferry. Immediately the burly man built a rough craft of planks and logs. He cleared a road from the northern gate to the Pootatuck, joining it upstream where the river narrowed. Then he cleared a landing site on the opposite shore in a sandy cove of cattails. At a half-penny per person, and two pence per horse and beast, he provided himself with a modest income and the colony with a necessary service.

One could now travel overland to Hartford, as well as by ship up the Sound.

Relatives and friends had arrived from England over the years, gradually increasing the population of Stratford. New industries grew. Shortly after settling in, Thomas Uffoot built a mill on a stream beyond the New Field. Robert Rice set up a tannery and Timothy Jackson a blacksmith's forge. Currier, cowkeeper, sheepmaster, leather-sealer—each found a place for a willing hand.

With such a steady stream of new settlers, the arrival of Charles Bassett received no special attention. The settlers were lost in their individual concerns.

The population had increased from within, too. Several marriages, sometimes cousin to cousin, had produced offspring. But the greatest excitement came in the fall of 1650. Goody Thomson announced that she was pregnant. "Imagine," she said. "After all these years!"

She was well into her forties, with two grown sons. The baby was due in the spring.

Goody Blakeman was ecstatic. "As Rachel said unto Jacob, 'Give me children or else I die!' "

"Genesis," Goody Thomson stated proudly. "Chapter 30, Verse 1!"

The news brought Anna Paine forth from her cabin, waking her as if from a dream. "See, thou! See, thou! She hath come late to childbearing, as I with my Ruth!"

For several days she would rise from her afternoon nap and stalk across the parade grounds, dogs barking at her heels, stopping everyone she encountered. "See, thou! Goody Thomson hath come late to childbearing!"

The townsfolk engaged the old woman in idle chatter until Ruth was sent for, to bring her home.

Ruth could usually be found at the ferry, floating back and forth across the Pootatuck, with Moses Wheeler at the tiller. It was her escape, her chance for quiet reflection.

Anna Paine had become senile. She was content to remain in her cabin, fueling the stone fireplace to boil water for no purpose, sweeping the dirt floor with a heavy straw broom until clouds of dust choked the air. The length of her midday naps had gradually increased until she slept for most of the afternoon. Ruth watched quietly until her breathing was deep and steady, then hastened from the cabin to the path that led to the ferry.

Moses Wheeler, on the job, was seldom talkative. Happy for the company, he sat cross-legged with his back to the tiller, a jug of cider between his knees, taking frequent sips as the ferry floated midstream. Even when no one hollered across from the far shore, he would give Ruth a ride, drifting from the wooded shadows of the near bank toward the distant reedy shallows. Such inattention often landed him far below his mark, but the big man never seemed to mind. He would laugh, swig his jug, and reach for his pole.

"Someday," he said, pointing a thick finger at the far bank, "ye'll find a turnpike from here to Hartford."

Ruth didn't answer. The autumn sun warmed her face. She lay across the bound, uneven logs and trailed her hand in the water. Not a cloud broke the solid blue sky.

How Stratford had changed! she thought. And she with it! What would the future bring? How many years of tending to Widow Paine?

She wasn't complaining. The widow had raised her. But it had been years since she had called her Mama.

Her thin limbs rested uncomfortably on the hard planks as she studied the big, bearded man at the tiller.

Papa Paine had been as tall and broad as Moses Wheeler, she remembered, and the widow was squat and square. How could the two of them have produced such a slender swamp reed as herself for an offspring?

Consider the noses. Papa's had been large and bulbous, a perfect potato. The widow's was short and stubby, almost the nose of a pig. Why was her own, then, so long and sharp?

And consider the hair. Papa's was as silky and fine as corn tassels—the color, if she remembered correctly, a dark brown. The widow's had always been a slate gray. From whence, then, her own coarse, red crop?

And her breasts. They had never swelled beyond the size of

88 ◆ *The Stratford Devil*

crabapples, while the widow's—the thought caused Ruth to laugh aloud—were like the pumpkins that now flourished in the field.

"What be so funny?" Moses Wheeler inquired, lifting his jug.

"Tend to thy cider, sir," Ruth laughed, "and leave me to my thinking!"

Her thoughts turned to Captain Mason, to the unfriendly gestures of the Red Man, and to the wolf pack that now ravaged the night. The Pequannocks, it was said, broke the fences in the farthest fields so the wolves could find the White Man's livestock. The raids had become a habit.

But Ruth had long ago made her peace with the Red Man, long ago made her peace with the wolf. If the Red Man had taken Jonas Paine's life, he had saved *her* from a savage death. And a rust-red wolf pelt had kept her warm for ten long winters.

Charles Bassett, of Harvard College, was Stratford's first schoolmaster. His salary was thirty-six pounds per year. The Meeting House served as his classroom, and a small, plain room was added to the wall behind the pulpit to serve as his lodging. In his honor the Meeting House was given a stone fireplace and a plank floor.

Before his arrival the education of the children had been carried out in the home, the parents offering whatever instruction they were able when time allowed. Religious training was the responsibility of Deacon Wells, who drilled the children from the Bible on the Sabbath. In the fall of 1650, however, a new routine began: daily classes in the three R's, once the harvest was in.

A tall, handsome man with the soft belly of a scholar, Mr. Bassett wore a gray suit that had been tailored in London, its sleek tails as sharp as a barn swallow's. Large silver buckles bound his black shoes.

His first love was the meeting house bell and he rang it boldly the day he moved in, the moment he saw the long rope dangling from the rafters.

Ruth came running. The men were in the fields, women and children doing chores about the home-lots.

Mr. Bassett was shouting above the noise. "For the young man, heir to the past and maker of the future, I ring! For the teacher, who enlarges the mind and strengthens the will, I ring! For the preacher of the fear of the Lord, the beginning of wisdom, I ring!"

Ruth stood in the open doorway out of breath, gazing across the rows of empty benches. Mr. Bassett didn't see her. He was about forty years of age, with sandy hair and salt-and-pepper sideburns. His upper lip, shaven clean, was bright pink. The dancing rope nearly took him from the floor.

"For the scholar who preserves learning, I ring! For the philosopher who ennobles life, I ring! For the man of science who widens knowledge, I ring!"

High overhead the heavy brass bell of Derbyshire swung back and forth in a steady clamor. Perspiration glistened on the schoolmaster's broad forehead. He hung on the rope like an excited child.

Ruth came forward and stopped beside the pulpit. At twenty-two she was tall, slim, and fiercely attractive. Her bright red hair, though tucked beneath a cap, escaped in wisps at the nape of her neck. A long, plain dress hid her feet.

Mr. Bassett looked up and the ringing halted abruptly. "Well, now. What have we here? Fair Venus, born of the foaming sea! Hast thou come from the Sound to my very door?"

Ruth met the bright look with a level stare. "Nay, sir. I be Ruth Paine and I come from the well, driven by thy insane tolling. I thought poor Sexton Peake had gone mad. He won't appreciate thy tune!"

Mr. Bassett took a large handkerchief from his breast pocket, unfolded it carefully, and wiped his brow. "I must find the proper knell for the schoolday. I admit my spirit is a bit carried away, but what a golden October afternoon! The very forests are aflame!"

"Aye, sir, and the caterpillars be as thick and furry as Reverend Blakeman's eyebrows, predicting a harsh winter to come!"

"The more reason to celebrate now." Mr. Bassett folded his handkerchief and tucked it neatly away. "Charles Bassett," he said with a short bow, "from Harvard College, Massachusetts Bay."

Ruth set her hands squarely on her hips, a habit acquired unconsciously from Widow Paine. "And do ye realize, sir," she interrupted, "even as ye madly sound thy bell, that Captain Mason treats with the Red Man? By the time the sun drops behind yon palisade, the wolves will howl in the fields! Such alarm as ye stir be not welcome in—"

The schoolmaster waved a finger. "Nay, Ruth Paine. The Indians and the wolves only serve to remind us of how much of the Lord's work remains to be done. 'In Adam's fall we sinned all.' That is our cross and we must bend to carry it."

Ruth was silent, her long tongue curling to her nose.

"I, for one, do not worry," the schoolmaster continued. "Stratford is defensible, is it not? Thy palisade is high and strong. Thy Sergeant Nichols seems to live for his train-band. I, for one, rarely leave my classroom, where I am surrounded by my books, protected by the knowledge of centuries. I am a wealthy man. I know none more fortunate. I have my lodging and thirty-six pounds per annum. What is there to fear in Stratford?"

Ruth shook her head. "But let an arrow trailing fire find the thatch of thy roof—"

"Nay, Venus. Let me ring my bell!" The long rope plunged downward and the bell sounded sharply. "For him who in letters interprets life, I ring! For him who in art beautifies life, I ring!"

Ruth turned from him and hurried down the aisle.

12.

The Agreement

INDIAN troubles now plagued the entire Connecticut Colony. In a bold move, Ansantaway, sachem of the Waramaugs, lay claim to the tribal lands east of the Pootatuck.

The General Court immediately denied his petition, refusing any hearing on the matter. The land was held as conquered, the Governor said, as a result of the Great Pequot War. Hadn't the Waramaugs fought beside the Pequots? Well then.

Fortunately for the settlers at Stratford, the Pootatuck provided a natural barrier between themselves and the people of Ansantaway. Rarely were Indians seen on the far shore, and Moses Wheeler, who crossed the river daily on his ferry, heard little of their activities from the travelers passing through. The Waramaugs, it was learned, were focusing their anger farther east, on the settlers of New Haven.

Upriver, far to the north, Towtanomow, sachem of the Paugassetts, also lay claim to native land. These ancient hunting grounds, he said, had been sacred for centuries. Though the Paugassetts had only trappers and traders to worry about, Towtanomow, like Ansantaway, feared for the future. He led his braves on occasional ambushes.

West of Stratford, the Pequannocks, following Ansantaway's lead, demanded the right of their hunting and fishing grounds at Cupheag. The boundaries that Captain Mason had established for Stratford—twelve miles along the Pootatuck to the

91

Sound, and eight miles to the west—had proved too large for the settlers to defend. Most of the ground lay unbroken. The fertile coastal land, the Captain admitted, was intended for future generations.

Queriheag himself, sachem of the Pequannocks, journeyed to Hartford to tell the General Court that the people of Stratford had no right to his territory. The General Court dismissed him as they had Ansantaway.

The Pequannocks fumed. Though war was out of the question—too costly, and impossible to win—they did neglect their tribute, withholding all wampum. And they annoyed the settlers whenever possible, within the limits of the White Man's patience.

In the worst of times, fire arrows flew over the palisade in the middle of the night, occasionally finding a thatched roof. But the small fires were doused by alert sentries, who formed a chain with ready buckets of rainwater.

Arrows came again on the Sabbath, disrupting the service. The women and children stayed safe in the Meeting House, the men clattered forth in a show of arms.

It was such circumstances that brought Captain Mason to Stratford in the fall of 1650. He had been to treat with the Pequannocks, for what he hoped would be the last time.

The settlers gathered on the riverbank. The day was unseasonably warm, too beautiful to be inside.

Ruth stood at a distance from the crowd. Although Captain Mason had visited Stratford on several occasions in the past years, she had not once gone forth to meet him. This was the man who could have spared the life of her Papa had he been more patient in the Great Pequot War.

He was as huge as Moses Wheeler, very portly in his advanced age, but his large brown eyes were bright and youthful. He wore buckskin from head to foot.

"Here is the agreement," the Captain shouted, "so newly

signed!" He unrolled a stiff length of parchment and held it high. "May it put an end to ten years of insufferable annoyances!"

The crowd cheered.

Captain Mason read in a deep bass voice: " 'Whereas there hath been a difference between the Indians of Pequannock and the inhabitants of Stratford, the Indians aforesaid acknowledging their former irregular carriage and misdemeanor and promising reformation in the particulars hereafter mentioned. . . .' " the Captain's voice drifted out over the riverbank.

Pausing to catch his breath, he glanced about at his audience. Several gulls hung motionless above the river, as if to listen. Reverend Blakeman nodded at Nicolas Knell.

" 'The Indians do hereby engage not to kill or anyway molest our cattle and swine. They engage to meddle with none of our corn, or peas to steal from us.' " The Captain went on, listing the promises the Pequannocks had made. Then he finished:

" 'The Indians aforesaid are well satisfied with what the committee has done, every particular, and have subscribed in the name of all the rest, this twenty-fourth day of October, 1650.

" 'Musquattat, his mark. Nesuposu, his mark. Pechekin, his mark. Nimrod, his mark. Queriheag, his mark!' "

A general shout rose from the riverbank.

"Praise the Lord!" Reverend Blakeman roared. "The sachem hath signed!"

"And the General Court," Captain Mason added with his fist in the air, "hath given leave that ye may prosecute!"

Another shout shot skyward, drowning the Captain's next words.

"Mr. Hawley shall make a true copy of this agreement, which I now post for thy perusal, to be kept in the Stratford Town Record!"

Turning aside, Captain Mason accepted a small hammer from Sergeant Nichols and ceremoniously tacked the document to the wall of the Meeting House. John Blakeman, in an iron hat and breastplate of the train-band, gave a sharp salute.

"Time to celebrate!" Moses Wheeler bellowed. He stood at the rear, closest to the riverbank, nearest to Ruth. "Let school be out for the day!" His cider jug swung on high.

Charles Bassett turned and glared above the sea of faces. The children cheered, hesitated, then ran off.

"Come now, Mr. Bassett," Moses Wheeler continued. "Let my jug be thine!"

Jane Blakeman, at her husband's side, frowned in her brother's direction. Directly behind her, Goody Thomson folded her hands over her womb, dreaming of the coming winter's confinement.

The crowd surged forward to examine the agreement on the wall. Nicolas Knell circled about to Moses Wheeler.

"Nay, sir. Be kind to the schoolmaster. We hear the children love him. America's future lies in the hands of such as he."

Mr. Bassett, by this time, had stormed into his empty school-room, ignoring the document tacked to the wall. The settlers lingered, discussing the agreement, and finally drifted off in a holiday mood.

Ruth paced on the riverbank impatiently. She was anxious to return home before Anna Paine woke up from her nap, but she wanted to examine the new document. One of the names read by Captain Mason had sent her back in time.

When the way was finally clear, she approached cautiously. There, near the bottom, just above the name of Queriheag, was the name of Nimrod.

" 'A mighty hunter before the Lord,' " Ruth said aloud.

His mark was simple: a pointed line suggesting an arrow beneath a curved line suggesting the horizon or the sun.

The marks of the others were less distinctive—like the queer imprints of chickens in the mud—except for Queriheag's: a dot within a circle, suggesting a watchful eye.

Ruth resisted an impulse to cry out. What had these ten years brought to Nimrod? she wondered. That bronze man with the tight black pigtail above the ear. The image she bore in her mind was eternal: cross-legged, arms folded on his chest, a leather pouch at his neck, pipe in mouth, and eyes as full as they were empty, fixed in a patient, peaceful stare.

Would he remember her? Did *he* fly his fire arrows across the palisade?

It pained her to think of him involved in any cause except the most noble.

A long shadow appeared on the wall beside her own. She turned quickly.

"It be displayed long enough," Goodman Hawley said. "It be time for copying. The Captain takes the original to Hartford in the morning."

Before he could raise his arm to remove the agreement, Ruth stood on tiptoe and pressed her lips to Nimrod's name.

13.

The Lecture Day

AT first, no one spoke of the wolves. What was there to say? They remained a mystery, invisible and unknown, except for those occasions when, in the light of midday, they sat boldly on their haunches at the edge of the woods and stared at the livestock through large yellow eyes.

At such moments, with the autumn sun leaning at an angle, their coats gleamed rust-red, dark brown, silver gray. They seemed the most grand and glorious creatures.

Unlike the Red Man, there was no way for the settlers to treat with the wolves, no way to understand their activities except by the silent evidence left the following morning.

Those marks in the mud along the postern gate: had the wolves come *that* close last night, to the very edge of the palisade? There had been no noise, no howling. But the settlers had learned to welcome the howling, because it meant the wolves were not on the move.

By light of day they examined the tracks: the large pad, the four toes, the four long claws, a full five inches from front to back.

At dusk, within the palisade, the settlers' dogs grew restless. Some of the Stratfordites, newly arrived, had brought with them large mastiffs thirty inches high at the shoulder, with drooping jowls, ugly lips, and thick skin that bunched in folds along their necks.

One evening, under orders from Reverend Blakeman, the dogs were set loose. "Let them scout the savage marauders," he said defiantly, "and teach them we mean to stay!"

The field spaniels ached to go too, running about excitedly, twitching their tails. But their short legs and bodies had been bred to hunt ground birds. They were no match for the power of the wolf.

The postern gate opened and the mastiffs ran off, barking loudly, straight for the dark woods.

Within minutes the barking turned to yelping, the yelping to whines. In the silence that followed, no dogs returned.

Reverend Blakeman was astounded. In England, the mastiffs had run the wolves out of Derbyshire.

"Irish wolfhounds be the answer," Nicolas Knell said.

Reverend Blakeman shook his head and retired to his study.

The Lecture Day, when Reverend Blakeman addressed his flock about the wolves, came as no surprise. It had been expected; many thought long overdue. The first frost had come and gone, crippling the pumpkin vines, freezing the wolf tracks in the thick mud.

The settlers pressed into the benches of the Meeting House. It was Saturday afternoon, and the children attended too.

Goodman Hawley inverted the hourglass, and the congregation stood. Reverend Blakeman entered in a hurry, his black frock coat flying, his broad white collars shining.

He wasted not a word.

"It be better to keep the wolf out of the fold than to trust to drawing his teeth and claws after he hath entered! It is a beast of waste and desolation! A fierce, bloodsucking persecutor of all that is high-born in man! A symbol of a savage and unholy wilderness!"

He gripped the front of the pine pulpit with both hands, leaning forward as his dark eyebrows danced.

"The very name of wolf be rooted in Satan! *Lupus*! How close to *lucem ferre*, 'to bear the light,' the contraction of which gives us Lucifer, the fallen angel!"

The congregation sat immobile, staring straight ahead. The words came almost as a relief, a public expression of their own worst fears.

"The wolf devours man's soul!" the Reverend exclaimed. "The shepherd drives the wolf from the sheep's throat, for which the sheep thanks the shepherd as liberator."

Ruth, beside Moses Wheeler on the last bench, blinked hard and bit her lip. Powerful memories stirred within her.

The white sand of Ipswich fell freely through the brassbound hourglass, its flow as steady as the Reverend's words.

"A sad thing is a wolf in the fold! As we read in Jeremiah, Those who have broken the yoke of the Lord: 'a wolf of the evenings shall spoil them.'

"How is it, brethren, that we deserve such punishment? Examine thy conscience, each and all!"

The Reverend was perspiring profusely.

How tall he looks in the pulpit, Ruth thought. How funny he looks when he stands beside his wife, the handsome Goody Blakeman an inch or two taller!

Moses Wheeler folded his arms across his chest.

"As Paul said to the Ephesians on the occasion of his last farewell: 'After my departing shall grievous wolves enter in among you, not sparing the flock.' "

Goodman Hawley turned the hourglass, and the lecture continued. The thumping overhead indicated a change of guard.

In the late afternoon, the Reverend concluded.

"The New World is a barren desert, an insult to the Lord! We are charged to make a fruitful field of the howling wilderness, to bring daylight to the darkness of the swamp! But there shall be no light without, my brethen, until there be light *within*!

"It be a hard winter when one wolf eats another!

"The wolf must die in his own skin!"

• • •

Charles Bassett, hurrying from the crowd on the riverbank, caught up with Ruth by the stocks and whipping post. Reaching out, he took her lightly by the arm.

The sunlight had thinned. The day was no longer bright or warm.

"Fair Venus, why do ye flee on Lecture Day?"

Ruth was startled, her thoughts already home ahead of her. Was Widow Paine up from her nap? Had she begun to wander, finding Ruth not there?

"The Reverend scolds us severely, sir."

The schoolmaster smiled. "Generations to come will look back to this hour and these scenes, to this day of small things, and say, 'Here was our beginning as a people! These were our fathers and mothers! Through their trials, we inherit our blessings.' "

Ruth quickened her pace. "According to Reverend Blakeman, the hand of God directs our every act."

"And so it does, and so it has, since the Fall of Man. The wolves be but evidence of original sin, but that sin shall be purged, together with the Indians and the wolves."

Ruth shook her head. "The wolves come to the Sound from the inland hills in search of a lazy living. They are creatures of nature. They take the easiest way."

"As does mankind, fair Venus, does he not? God's plan be divine and—"

"I worry only for my mother, Mr. Bassett."

"As, yes, the Widow Paine, thy *mother*. And you, her—*waif*."

"But you insult me, sir."

"I know only what I hear, fair Venus, for you make such a habit of avoiding me."

"I don't apologize. My time is spoken for."

"Aye, wasted midstream in the Pootatuck."

"Nay, sir. Those be sacred moments. All else be—"

"Wasted with a drunken ferry keeper."

Ruth shook her elbow free. The two figures hurried side by side.

"Moses Wheeler is the backbone of Stratford, sir. Even now he runs to our home-lot to pack mud and leaves about the cabin, to ensure us extra warmth against the coming winter."

Mr. Bassett strained to keep up. He suddenly seemed ashamed. "My duty in Stratford is to teach the children."

"Then wherefore not *all* the children?" Ruth turned and looked at him. "Deliverance and Mary Blakeman and Humility Wells be the only girls—"

"Learning is not necessary for women. The skills of the home be more than enough."

"Is that why the Englishwoman came to the New World? To sit at home and work her fingers stiff? To weave delicate traceries on an embroidery frame?"

Mr. Bassett whipped his handkerchief from his coat pocket and wiped his brow. "The Englishwoman came with her husband, fair Venus."

"And was he the only reason? Did none come because of a sense of adventure? Of their own free will?"

Charles Bassett halted abruptly at the head of the narrow path that led to the log cabin in the corner of the palisade. "Ruth Paine," he said loudly, "thou art an uncivilized and headstrong child of America, blind to its true mission and blind to thyself!"

Moses Wheeler looked up as he circled the cabin with a bucket of leaves and mud. Ruth waved to him and walked ahead.

Had she turned to look behind her as the schoolmaster departed, she would have seen John Blakeman moving quickly from oak to oak.

14.

Mr. Pervis

DIRECTLY after the Sabbath service, Reverend Blakeman tacked a stiff broadside to the wall of the Meeting House. With old Nicolas Knell at his side, he read aloud to the congregation huddled before him on the riverbank.

" 'Whereas great loss and damage doth befall the plantation of Stratford by reason of wolves, which destroy great numbers of our livestock, it is ordered by this plantation, and the authority thereof, that any person who shall kill a wolf or wolves, within ten miles of the bounds of Stratford, shall have for every wolf by him so killed, ten shillings paid out of the treasurie, provided that due proof be made thereof.' "

The Reverend turned to the anxious faces that greeted his words. "This announcement shall be copied by Goodman Hawley and sent forthwith to Hartford, where the General Court shall make it known throughout the Connecticut Colony, that Stratford shall pay for dead wolves!"

By the end of November, an early winter seemed certain. The wind had increased, sweeping in from the Sound. Snow squalls swirled up the Pootatuck. The days had grown shorter, the trees were stripped bare, the distant woods a black and purple band.

At night the wind whipped through the palisade, driving hard against the thick cabin walls. As if sensing the growing cold would mean a famine, the wolves ranged wide in reckless slaughter. In five weeks, only two had been killed.

Then suddenly, one afternoon, the whitecaps left the Sound, the choppy waves flattened on the Pootatuck. The sun burned away the wintry grayness and, for a few hours at least, Stratford stood bright and warm.

The settlers came forth without their heavy woolen cloaks to stroll on the parade grounds.

"God hath given us," the Reverend said, "this one last day, to sustain our spirits through the bleak months ahead. Let us bask in its light—in *His* light!"

The settlers cheered. Mr. Bassett brought his classes outside. Nicolas Knell leaped high and kicked his heels.

Ruth ran immediately to the river, the Widow Paine asleep, to join Moses Wheeler at his ferry. Sitting back to back, they soon drifted midstream, the long-handled tiller unattended.

Large gulls floated high overhead, flocks of terns skimming the water, rising abruptly at the edge of the marshes, as if in sport.

Ruth faced to the east, studying the landing. No one waited to be ferried across. There was nothing there but the sandy inlet, the stiff, still cattails, and the wide meadows giving way to distant hills.

Behind her lay the wooded shore of Stratford, thick with brown leaves that even the sun couldn't brighten. Downstream, far to her right, the Pootatuck joined the Sound, the Meeting House bell tower rising above the graveyard on the riverbank.

Upstream, the river narrowed like a watery arrow, coming to a point within the heart of the rolling woodland. Ruth had been there once, and she remembered.

Moses Wheeler sipped his jug and shook his head. "Thy shoulderblades be knifeblades for sure, Ruth Paine, good for slicing apples as well as my back!"

"Nay, Mr. Wheeler. Let me enjoy the day without my cloak. After this ye won't feel my shoulders 'til spring!"

Moses Wheeler roared and raised his jug.

The crude craft hardly left a wake. There was no lap or splash about the logs. Ruth held her face to the sun.

"I think," she said after a while, "that we do not prize our happiness here as we have cause."

"And never will, with the wolf at our gate."

"Do ye figure the Pequannocks to hunt for the bounty?"

"Good God Gravy, no! Queriheag agreed to nothing respecting wolves. The wolves do the sachem a service!"

Ruth looked again to the landing site, the blue water sparkling.

"The wolves come to Stratford, Mr. Wheeler, because we are here. We open the gate ourselves."

"Aye, with the help of the Pequannocks," Moses Wheeler laughed. "But ye speak the truth, child. The wolves are as intelligent as our Mr. Bassett. They must provide for their own. We offer fat cattle."

"It is just as Nimrod told Stanton," Ruth said to herself, "so many years ago."

The ferry keeper reached for the tiller. "What, child?"

"I said that I, for one, do not fear the wolf. I have looked the wolf in the eye."

Moses Wheeler laughed again. "If ye have, young lady, it were well not to tell the Reverend!"

Ruth stared at the shore again, where the blue of the river rippled against the yellow sand. Turning her head suddenly, she caught the ferry keeper's gaze.

"Now tell me, Mr. Wheeler, and tell me truly. Are ye never lonely in Stratford?" The theme, somehow, had entered her head.

"Lonely? Good God Gravy, child! Timothy Jackson lacks shingles for his roof, and my sister wants cupboards in the kitchen. Families wait to trade log cabins for new frame dwellin's. And if I didn't tend to this tiller, little lady, this ferry would find its way to Sewenhacky. Lonely? No, child, not when there's work to be done. Work is the Lord's way of preventin' loneliness."

Ruth trailed her hand in the water. "I have heard the Reverend speak often of the rewards of labor, sir, and I have labor enough in caring for my—for Widow Paine. But have ye never wanted for a partner, sir? Have ye never wanted for a wife?"

Moses Wheeler fixed his jug between his feet, nodding and smiling. "Aye, child. I fathom thy drift. So let me tell thee that, before we sailed from England, there were a young woman about thine own age. As pretty a little thing as ever seen on God's green earth. She was the daughter of a merchant in Ipswich. And let me tell thee, too, child, she held a soft spot in her heart for young Moses Wheeler. But her father were Lord Mayor and given to politickin' for the king. So when plans were laid to come to the New World, there were no doubt what Moses Wheeler would do. I asked her to sail with us, to marry me once we had settled the land. Her father suspected. I were but a poor carpenter, and so—"

"She refused."

"Aye, Ruth. She refused. She were trained to obey. Sometimes I think on her when I float out here alone, but thy company helps to keep her tucked away in the back of my thick brain. I don't dwell on it, but . . ." Moses Wheeler seemed to want to drop the subject. "What about thee, Ruth? Be there no one to hold thy heart?"

It was Ruth's turn to laugh. "Not within the bounds of Stratford, sir."

"I think our Reverend's son, John—"

"John Blakeman is as haughty as his mother."

Moses Wheeler roared. "Aye, child! If my sister has a fault, it be her pride."

"And he is given to impolite stares."

"The boy's feelin' his nutmeg, Ruth, is all. But what of our schoolmaster, Mr. Bassett? Now there's a—well, a bit of a dandy, really, but—"

"Mr. Bassett bears his learning like a crown, sir. He can't speak unless to a student. I am not one for books, Mr. Wheeler. And yet I would learn."

Ruth hesitated. The current swelled beneath her. Suddenly she wanted to tell Moses Wheeler everything—about the eyes she often saw in the woods, about the dark fires they stirred within her; the entire truth of what she'd ever thought and felt. She looked away, however. There was someone on the shore, a slim reed of a man waving a large white rag.

She jerked a sharp elbow into Moses Wheeler's thick side. "Traveler, sir! It's time you were a-work!"

The burly man leaped to the tiller and the raft began to move, catching the slow pull of the current. Ruth stood on the flat planking and gave a tentative wave.

On shore, the slim man put his white flag away. A large burlap sack sat beside him in the sand, not smooth and flat like the sacks at Mr. Uffoot's new grist mill, but stiff and angular like the stranger himself. The man seemed tensed, ready to spring, like the snares the Red Man set for small game.

Once he had caught their attention, he had looked down, ignoring all but the sack at his feet.

Slanting in from the west, the sun struck the shallow landing area in a dazzling shimmer. Of course, Ruth thought. That is why he does not look up: the sun is straight in his eyes.

The ferry glided in, crunching through brittle cattails a few yards short of its mark, and in one swift motion the stranger swung his sack aboard, even before the craft had grounded.

The planks shook with a heavy clanking thud, as if struck by a ship's anchor chain. Ruth stared at the strange cargo.

Then the stranger himself sprang aboard. He was about fifty years of age, tall, slim, with a flushed, pockmarked face half hidden by a ragged red beard. A red woolen cap topped his head.

The man bent over his sack. His gray knee-stockings were thick with round burrs and his leather britches caked with mud. The long sleeves of his gray shirt showed skin at the elbow. Even for the sun-filled day, the shirt could not have been warm enough.

He pulled his red cap down over his ears. Large freckles blotched the skin on the back of his hands.

"Be that Stratford?" he said finally. His voice was rusty. Squinting severely, he looked up for the first time, not at Ruth or Moses Wheeler, but at the distant shore.

"Aye, sir. That be Stratford."

"Then take me across."

Ruth retreated a step or two, toward the tiller.

"And this be Ruth," Moses Wheeler said. "And I be Moses."

"Pervis," the man said, as if distracted. He kicked his sack, the metal sounding within, then sat down.

He pointed at the jug at Ruth's feet. "Cider?"

"Used to be," Moses Wheeler said. "It's stronger now."

"Then I'll be havin' some. Too long since I've held such a jug."

Moses Wheeler leaned against the tiller and nodded his head. Ruth took the jug and offered it at arm's length.

When the ferry struck the Stratford shore, the stranger was still drinking. Then the jug was set aside and the huge sack flew to the riverbank, clanging and banging as it landed in the leaves. Its owner leaped ashore behind it.

"Ha' penny per person," Moses Wheeler said.

The stranger smiled—or winced—reaching downward. "A ha' penny would make me a rich man, Mr. Moses. Ye'll be paid triple within a week. Ye have my word."

The huge sack clanked to the man's back, and without another word, he loped away toward the settlement.

An hour later, as Ruth hurried home in the yellow glow of

late afternoon, she found an excited crowd milling about the parade ground.

"Can ye believe it?" Goody Thomson said, her hands crossed on her swelling white apron. "Come on such a day to deliver us!"

"Didn't my Adam proclaim this day a gift of God?" Goody Blakeman said, shaking the leaves from a picnic blanket.

Ruth lowered her eyes as she passed a circle of menfolk —Reverend Blakeman, Sergeant Nichols, Nicolas Knell—and pretended not to hear their words.

"How fortunate," the Reverend said, "his heavy sack made such a noise, frightening the wolves long enough for him to climb a tree. The Lord was with him, to bring him to our side!"

Young John Blakeman joined his father. "What a timely saviour, this bounty hunter!" He kept his eyes on Ruth as she passed.

"To think he watched his horse eaten alive!"

"Nay," said Nicolas Knell, "it be certain this man has seen worse than that!"

"He told *me*," Sergeant Nichols said, "that wolves are amiable, rompin' with their pups, pouncin' on one another while they nap. He said they even play tag with the crows!"

"And prance about with bones in their mouths! Can ye believe it, the same wolves that eat our dogs?"

"Mr. Pervis is a man of business," the Reverend said. "He knows the wolf. The Lord be praised for sending him to Stratford, in the hour of our need!"

Ruth hurried away, quickening her pace, as Charles Bassett stepped from the group of men. He had caught her eye. He seemed to have something to say.

But where was this Pervis, this man of the wolves?

Opening the door to her cabin moments later, Ruth found him sitting on the nail keg, smoothing her rust-red pelt across his knees.

15.

The Wolf Man

PERVIS was running his fingers back and forth across the wolf pelt, ruffling the fur, then laying it smooth.

Anna Paine slept soundly in the far corner beneath a coarse woolen blanket, her face turned to the log wall. The cabin was extremely warm. Despite the unseasonable day, the widow had insisted on loading the fireplace with dry logs, setting them ablaze before taking her nap.

And despite the heat, Pervis still had his red knit cap pulled down about his ears.

"The finest I've seen," he said without looking up. "The skinnin' were perfect. The curin' too. Not a hair lost." His rusty voice came so deliberately, and with such respect, that Ruth could only stand in the open doorway, her hands on her hips.

"The children were excited," Pervis continued. "The schoolmaster let 'em show me the latest tracks at the north gate. Then I asked about lodgin' and they laughed. 'The Widow Paine be needin' company,' they said. They pointed here. The door were unbarred. When I came on in, they stopped laughin' and ran away."

Pervis flipped the pelt to its yellow underside, tracing his finger along the smooth inner edge. "Like shammy," he said. "A perfect cure." He shook his head. "But there'll be no time for curin' when I set about my work. It don't pay. Carcasses is all they want."

Ruth looked behind her. The air had chilled and the day

grown dark. The parade grounds were suddenly deserted. The oak trees stood tall and empty in the grainy blackness.

She closed the door, eyes leaping about the room. Where was his sack, the strange man's burlap sack?

Her bed stood neat and tidy to her right, a pine frame and straw mattress made by Moses Wheeler. Had Pervis slid his sack beneath it? Did he intend to stay?

Sitting down at the edge of her bed, she glanced under the frame. There was nothing there but the bare dirt floor.

"The schoolmaster sent one of the urchins back to say that Ruth would be along directly." Pervis spoke as if there had been no interruption, his eyes on the pelt. "I said to tell the schoolmaster that we met on the ferry." As he spoke, tight creases spread from the corners of his deep-set eyes, and for an instant Ruth was certain he was an Indian.

A Red Man.

But unlike the Red Man he had a scraggly beard, his nose was sharp and thin, his name was Pervis, and he had come from— from whence?

"When I see a pelt like this," the wolf man said, "I am reminded that the wolf is basically a coward: shy, timid, curious perhaps, and most certainly intelligent, yet basically a coward." He smiled—or winced—briefly. "Now try tellin' that to Reverend Blakeman."

He kept his eyes on the wolf pelt.

Ruth glanced about anxiously, first to the fireplace, then to the Widow Paine, and to the front door. Then she looked up into the rafters directly above Pervis, into the square dark space that led to the shallow loft. A corner of the burlap sack hung from the opening, like the tongue of a cow.

So it was true! He intended to stay!

How had that sack landed above without its noisy clanking waking Widow Paine?

Ruth's thoughts fled like startled birds. "This be no boarding house!" she said jumping up. Her hands planted themselves sharply on her hips. She felt giddy, the cabin too warm.

"It'll do," Pervis said slowly. "It's out of the way, and close by the north gate. I can't be about my work with children underfoot."

Still, he did not look up. His scruffy eyebrows seemed like fluffs of milkweed, about to blow away in the slightest breeze.

Why didn't he remove that red knit cap?

Ruth was speechless.

"And before I forget, I bring ye a greetin'."

"What, sir? To *me*?"

"If ye be Ruth Paine."

"Aye, sir—"

"Tommy Stanton bids Hello from Hudson's River."

Ruth lay awake, unable to sleep. She wrapped the wolf pelt more closely about her. The cold winds had resumed, the warmth gradually leaking from the cabin.

Pervis had climbed from the nail keg to the narrow storage space of the loft and fallen asleep immediately. Anna Paine had got up for a bit of porridge, then returned to bed, unaware of her—her *guest*?

Her boarder.

In the morning, Ruth would try to explain.

Leaves swirled about outside, rushing at the walls of the cabin, rattling above the thatch. The palisade creaked in the wind. The warm afternoon seemed a dream.

Imagine! Pervis had met Mr. Stanton at Hudson's River! The old Indian interpreter, "Mr. Many Tongues"—the 'bald eagle,' as Pervis called him—trading news of the bounty hunt in Stratford! Winter had struck hard in the north territories, the trapping poor, so Pervis had headed south immediately.

Ruth had all but forgotten Thomas Stanton. In the ten long years since her Pootatuck journey, her memories had centered on Nimrod, that noble savage who had come to her aid. As a girl, she had never understood why Mr. Stanton hadn't returned with her to Stratford. As a woman, she understood all too well. Vicious rumors still linked her name to Sergeant Nichols. Mr. Stanton had wisely remained on neutral ground, as he did when he brought the White Man and Red Man together.

So Stanton remembered her and sent his greetings! What else had he told Pervis? she wondered. Was that wolf man and his sack really up there in that square dark hole in the rafters?

Ruth rolled over, wrestling with the wolf pelt, her long red hair tangled in the strings of her nightcap. Finally, when dawn approached, she fell asleep.

The sun rose over the river not long after, its yellow light glowing through the oiled cloth of the window. An ax sang in the woods beyond the palisade, clear and vibrant in the cold morning air.

When the yellow light reached Ruth's face, her eyes opened. Immediately she looked to the loft. The corner of the burlap sack no longer hung from the opening. Pervis was gone.

Then she heard the chopping in the woods.

Anna Paine rolled over, snoring loudly, her face to the door. In a moment the spreading light would reach her eyes.

Ruth swung her feet to the cold dirt floor. A small fire crackled with fresh logs on top. The nail keg had been set beneath the window, and in front of the fireplace lay a collection of metal traps neatly arranged in two short rows.

The crude instruments were horseshoe shaped. They looked like sets of teeth that didn't quite mesh. They were forged from bog iron, old scythe blades, and old files. The frames and crosspieces seemed hammered from blacksmith scraps, the springs fashioned from the long, thin rods used for ramming shot down the barrel of a musket.

Clutching her woolsey bedclothes to her chest, Ruth crossed the room. The traps were warm to the touch, heated by the morning fire. The teeth were not sharp, but their bite, she imagined, would be ferocious.

There were eight traps in all, four in each row. Some were

larger than others. Kneeling beside them, Ruth inspected each one.

The chopping continued in the woods.

Anna Paine stirred, rolled to the wall, and resumed snoring. Ruth stood suddenly, noticing something on the nail keg beneath the window.

Stepping closer, she saw a necklace. A perfect circle of wolves' teeth. Each tooth was triangular, sharp, and as large as a thumb.

She extended a finger and immediately withdrew it, too afraid to touch. What a contrast to the metal teeth by the fireplace! Such a grotesque ornament! Such a string of beauty!

All the teeth were the eye teeth, the fangs of the wolf, the same fangs that, ten long years ago, had left four scars at the top of her leg.

How many wolves had been killed to make this necklace?

She began to count, but Anna Paine awoke.

Pervis returned at noon, long enough to trade his ax for a spade. The wind had stopped, the day bright but much colder than the day before. "The stakes be done," he said to Ruth, meeting her outside the cabin. "Time to dig." His red knit cap and thin shirt were dark with sweat.

"I told my mother you were come for the wolves," Ruth said. "She has not answered. You must realize, sir, that she—"

"The necklace is for you," Pervis interrupted.

"What?"

"On the wooden keg. My gift. In a few days' time I'll pay thee further in shillings." They stood before the cabin, Pervis on his way to the northern gate. "The Red Man would trade his squaw for such a string."

Ruth looked over her shoulder to the open cabin door. "The teeth of *mogke-oaas*," she said quietly.

"Ah, so you know the wolf!"

Ruth shook her head.

"The Red Man believes the wolf's spirit resides in its teeth. Wear them and the wolf walks with you." Pervis scratched at the caked dirt on the spade.

Ruth shook her head again sharply. "We are forbidden to wear baubles, sir. No lace, no ruffles, no silk; only the plainest cloth to—"

"Winter comes, Ruth Paine, does it not? Ye dress in layers. Wear the teeth next to thy skin. Next to thy heart."

Anna Paine suddenly appeared in the open doorway, a puzzled look on her face, her broad apron wrinkled and soiled. She held aloft a thick straw broom, as if to brush cobwebs from the sky.

"I must go," Ruth said.

"Don't wait up tonight on my account."

Pervis headed for the northern gate, the spade on his shoulder like a musket. He kept his eyes on the frozen turf as the settlers hurried to their home-lots for the midday meal.

16.

The Pit

SINCE the wolves continued to slaughter the livestock, all cattle, sheep, and hogs were confined to small pens and paddocks outside the palisade. Although the harvest had been a good one, the livestock was crucial. A severe winter and hungry wolves would mean a test of survival as harsh as Sandy Hollow's first year.

Pervis dug the pit where the wolf trails came together, by a scent post at the edge of the New Field. The huge hole was dug in the shape of an ink pot—wider at the bottom than across the top—to prevent the wolves from climbing up the sides. Lacy roots lined the walls, eight feet deep.

Digging farther into the sandy bottom, Pervis erected a grid-work of a dozen upright stakes, slimmer and sharper than those that formed the palisade.

No one watched him work. The harvest was in and the settlers prepared for winter within the palisade, repairing plows, splitting wood, and filling the chinks about the windows and walls. Some spent the afternoon at the beach below the bluffs, digging for clams and mussels in the heavy wet sand. The children continued at school, with most of the young girls remaining at home to help their mothers, to polish the pewter and brass, and learn how to knit.

In all private conversations, however, there was whisper of the wolf man.

After supper Ruth left the cabin door unbarred, a larger blaze than usual in the fireplace. The traps remained as Pervis had left them, but the necklace had been claimed.

Ruth set a plate of cold pork pie on the nail keg for the wolf man, and went to bed as soon as darkness fell, exhausted by the previous night's lack of sleep.

When Pervis returned from his digging, all the homes in the settlement were dark. He moved about the cabin quietly, heating water in the large kettle above the fire. A shallow wooden tub lay in front of his traps.

Coarse blankets arched above Anna Paine like an Indian burial mound. In the opposite corner, only the tip of Ruth's white nightcap stuck from her wolf pelt.

Propping himself against the nail keg, Pervis kicked off his buckskin boots. Methodically he plucked the round, sticky burrs from his knee-stockings and tossed them, one by one, into the fire. The little balls blazed briefly, then shrunk to black ash.

He tugged off his stockings. Raising his arms, he drew his shirt over his head without removing his red knit cap.

Standing quietly, he untied the rawhide drawstring about his waist and in one quick move stepped from his britches and smallclothes.

Anna Paine mumbled and rolled over, deep in sleep.

Pervis folded his garments and set them neatly on the nail keg. Stepping lightly over his traps, he lifted the huge black kettle from its hanging iron in the fireplace. It was the water striking the tub that woke Ruth.

She turned her head ever so slightly and opened an eye.

What was this apparition standing before the fireplace, shrouded in a mist of rising steam? His back was to her, his buttocks hollow and drawn, his spine a rippling line of question marks. Like his traps, his joints seemed crude and ill-fitted.

Pervis stooped in the tub, soaping his body, and Ruth shuddered. She had never seen a naked man before.

Stepping from the tub, his backside to the fire, the wolf man rubbed himself vigorously, hopping in place, red knit cap still on his head.

Ruth shut her eyes and shuddered again. What great sin had here been committed! What abomination! What horrid naked-ness!

A dog barked in the middle of the parade grounds, sharp yelps from a feisty field spaniel. A second answered faintly from the postern gate.

Ruth looked again.

Pervis was kneeling over the tub, his head sunk in the water. As he raised himself up, she saw a white blaze on his scalp. It ran from forehead to crown, right through the middle of his wet hair. She stared at the smooth stretch of a massive scar.

Soapy water dripped from the wolf man's beard into the tub. The hot soaking had left his face as red as his hair.

When he dunked his head again, Ruth squeezed her eyes shut, unable to look further.

Rising early in the morning of the third day, Pervis set his smallest trap in the tall grass beyond the edge of the New Field, baited with wilted turnip greens. Within an hour he snagged a white-tailed rabbit.

Flaying the carcass, he set it aflame in the bottom of the pit.

The greasy smoke rose quickly, blown into the woods by a brisk breeze from the Sound. The gaping hole was then covered with brush and straw.

All afternoon, while the odor of burnt meat spread through the woods, Pervis was at work in a corner of the Old Field, chopping stakes and digging another pit. The wolf tracks were thick there, too.

At dusk the wind shifted, turning in the direction of the palisade, and suddenly the sheep began to bleat. The cows bumped one another in their pens, and the hogs rooted madly in the mud.

The excited animals drew a crowd to the paddocks. Then the

settlers raced across the New Field to where Pervis already stood before his pit. His arms were folded, his eyes trained below.

The setting sun stood like a red plate on the black treetops to the west. The settlers huddled around the pit, as at a grave.

The wolf, a large silver-gray, had caught the stake beneath the jaws as it fell. It had died instantly without a sound, the stake finding its brain.

"Good God Gravy!" Moses Wheeler exclaimed. He had left his ferry early, hoping to witness such an event.

"Stop the children," Nicholas Knell said.

Sexton Peake backed away from the edge of the pit and halted the flock of youngsters at mid-field. "Return home!" he yelled. "Forbidden to look!" He waved his arm like his Sabbath switch.

"Nay!" Reverend Blakeman shouted. "Let them gaze!"

Ruth came running, Mr. Bassett at her side. As they reached the pit, the schoolmaster pointed at Pervis and whispered to her, "Such a dark force cannot overcome chaos. Such a dark force only makes the chaos blacker!"

Ruth ignored him, wedging in by Moses Wheeler to look in the pit.

She saw only the teeth, the magnificent bared teeth, frozen in mid-air like the teeth of that dreamy afternoon so long ago.

The children shrieked.

"The very painting of Hell!" the Reverend exclaimed. "The yawning pit! The jaws of death! The fallen soul, skewered by its own self-serving greed! Gaze hard and well, my brethren, and remember Jeremiah! 'Those who have broken the yoke of the Lord: a wolf of the evenings shall spoil them'!"

Pervis looked through the gathering darkness to the Old Field. "I'll be needin' ten shillings," he said.

Long past midnight, Moses Wheeler stumbled across the parade grounds with Pervis slung over his shoulder, both men stinking drunk. The wolf man had paid in triple for his ferry ride, then purchased two jugs of cider, presenting one to the seller as a gift.

"Poison!" he cried loudly. He beat his fists on the big man's back, the fringe of his jacket flailing the black air. "Poison! Thine apples be worm-ridden!"

Moses Wheeler roared. "Sweetest drink this side of Sewen-hacky!"

"Pittoohey!"

"My ferry sits at the river and yet I ferry thee home!"

"Mind the oak, ye big oaf!"

"Bye and bye, Mr. Pit-worth. Bye and bye!"

Candles appeared in darkened windows, trailing the two men like a comet's tail. The spaniels barked at a distance and ran in circles, too frightened to venture closer.

At the Paines' cabin, Moses Wheeler missed the front step, and Pervis flew into the wall. Both men roared, unhurt, too loose for injury.

"Mankind fell for an apple, Mr. Wheeler. Ain't that so? Ain't that what thy Reverend's book says?"

"Good God Gravy! The truth be told!"

Laughter split the darkness. Ruth shuddered within. Then the cabin door flew open with a bang.

Pervis entered, a finger to his lips.

"Hush!" Moses Wheeler cried. "Wake not the widow, lest she club thee about the head with her broom!" The big man remained in the doorway, his body broad enough to block the cold night air.

Pervis crashed into his traps.

"Hush, Pit-worth!"

"Bye and bye, ye big oaf!"

Righting himself, he turned his buckskin pockets inside out, spilling half a dozen shillings in front of the fireplace.

"For bed and breakfast," he said loudly. "Witness, oaf: I be a man of my word!"

Turning, he pointed to the square dark space in the rafters.

Moses Wheeler fell forward as if the door frame had been holding him up. Catching Pervis by an arm and the seat of his pants, he spun him overhead like a wrestler.

"Mind the beams, oaf!"

"Bye and bye, Mr. Pit-worth! Bye and bye!"

Then the wolf man flew into the loft.

17.

The Bounty Hunt

PERVIS returned to the pit before sunrise, and as he expected, found a second wolf trapped within. A dark brown female, the mate of the first, had slipped over the far edge and caught two stakes, one in the chest, the other through the left rear flank. The animal lay twisting on the stakes until Pervis clubbed it to death with his spade.

Dragging the carcasses back to the palisade, he bound their hind feet with strips of rawhide and hung them from pegs on the rear wall of Anna Paine's log cabin. Then he hiked out to the Old Field to complete the second pit.

The day dawned cold, the clouds no longer the high, white clouds of autumn but thin and ribbed, forecasting winter. Within the palisade the settlers resumed the round of daily chores.

By nightfall, a flayed rabbit smoldered in the bottom of the new pit. In the morning, Pervis hung two more wolves on Anna Paine's wall.

Pervis dug a third pit beyond the northern gate, at the edge of the woods by the path to the ferry. Because of thick leaves, the area was free of tracks, but it was marked with definite patches of toenail scratchings. New scent posts suggested that the wolves were fanning out, ranging west from the river in a wide arc to the Sound, exploring every avenue to the livestock.

Covered with a flimsy screen of brush and leaves, the third pit soon reeked of burnt rabbit flesh.

Pervis returned to his collection of carcasses. Stiff with frost, the animals hung in an ever-growing row, drawing frequent spectators to the home-lot in the corner of the palisade. Annoyed by the visitors, Anna Paine stood on the stone front step, brandishing her broom, engaging in shouting matches, until Ruth could persuade the townsfolk to turn away.

Pervis worked silently out back, shooing the spaniels that came to growl at the wolves. Slitting each carcass through the stomach, he removed the bladder and anal glands and chopped them up with small pieces of bluish fat. Then he set the concoction aside to ripen.

Anna Paine never missed the wooden bowl he took from the log mantel, but she did begin to detect a strong odor about the cabin, sniffing constantly, waving her broom at the rafters to disperse the air.

When he went to set his traps several days later, Pervis took the mixture with him in a leather water bag. The traps had been scrubbed clean, scoured with sand from the bluffs until they shone and all traces of human scent were removed. He only touched them wearing cowhide gloves. The burlap sack had been buried in a cow manure to remove its scent. The coarse sack served as a setting cloth, spread over the ground whenever Pervis knelt to bed his traps.

He set the traps at water holes, at scent posts, at the intersections of trails, and at the grounds where the sheep had slept last summer. Wherever a carcass had lain for a length of time, a trap waited. Although the wolves roamed as much as sixty miles daily, they returned routinely to the site of rotted flesh.

The wolf scent was sprinkled from the leather water bag onto the traps. Spreading the burlap sack, Pervis knelt and dug away the soil with gloved hands, always favoring a slight depression in the earth so the wolf's full weight would be pressing forward as it hit the trap.

The shallow beds were only as wide and long as the traps

themselves. A square of deerskin was placed in each excavation and covered with loose, sandy soil. Then the trap was set in, jaws fixed open, and carefully concealed with dry leaves.

Whenever possible, Pervis entered and left the bedded areas by water, sloshing along the Pootatuck, through the brooks beyond the New Field, and through marshy bogs to the west of the bluffs. He set one trap in the middle of a stream, where a flat rock stuck out a few feet from shore. No digging was necessary. A flayed rabbit, sprinkled with wolf scent, was draped across the rock, the trap staked to the bottom of the streambed. The wolf would splash along the easiest path, moving to the carcass in the same intelligent steps as a man.

Cold winds shook the cabin. Anna Paine lay asleep in the far corner, Ruth and Pervis in front of the fire, Pervis on his nail keg, Ruth on her rust-red pelt.

"The Red Man calls the December moon The Moon When The Wolves Run Together. If it doesn't snow, I'll be a rich man by Christmas." The rusty voice was deliberate, unexcited, directed more to the yellow flames than to Ruth.

"And if it snows?"

"No hurry. Wolves bear their pups in the spring. I'll find the dens and dig 'em out. Little ones pay the same as big." Pervis plucked a round burr from his tattered knee-stocking and tossed it at the flames. Then he pulled his red knit cap about his ears.

"The Mohegans," he continued after a while, "call the wolf *mai-coh*. It means 'witch.' Whenever they kill one they hold a large ceremony to express regret and call the wolf 'friend.' They believe that to kill a wolf invites trouble from the others. So they shoot a fire arrow into the night sky to light the way to their feast. They don't want witches on their backs."

The flames glinted in the wolf man's deep-set eyes. Not once did he look up at Ruth.

"And do ye believe that?"

"I fear the Red Man more than witches or wolves." Pervis plucked another burr from his knee-stocking and twirled it between thumb and finger. "There be renegade Red Men and renegade wolves. And loafer Red Men and loafer wolves. Both are crafty. A wolf will stalk thee but never attack. Ye never know what a Red Man will do."

The sticky burr flew into the fire, and Ruth watched it curl to ash.

"Once the Red Man sets his mind on the scalp of a particular trapper, there's trouble ahead for weeks." Pervis scratched his thin eyebrows, which seemed to quiver. "He'll lie in ambush and force ye to slip back, to take a new trail. And just when ye think he's gone for good—whang! An arrow whizzes out of the woods. The Red Man would like nothin' better than to set yer head on a pike, to watch the skin sag from the cheekbones and the eyes fall back in the skull." Pervis paused, then seemed to sum up. "It's a game of wits. A wolf don't break the rules. The Red Man will."

Ruth crossed her legs beneath her heavy skirt, her long tongue curling to her nose. "When I was a girl," she said, "I saw trappers at the trading post in Windsor. I loved their spirit. They always seemed so . . . free."

Pervis smiled—or winced—briefly. "The white trapper is a trespasser," he said. "He must travel after nightfall. His horse must be well hobbled and never out of sight, lest it be stolen or take an arrow through the ears. In the north territories the trapper travels by canoe, keepin' to the shadows of the trees along the banks. The handle of his paddle must be wrapped in rags, to muffle the noise in case it strikes the gun'l." Pervis shook his head and seemed to laugh. "It's gray all day, and the cold hits like a hammer. A poor-strung snowshoe means freezin' to death. There be no thoughts of freedom. Ye'd starve."

The fire popped and spit. Anna Paine rolled over beneath her pile of blankets. Ruth stared straight at the yellow flames. Just beyond the warm stones of the fireplace, she realized, a dozen carcasses hung frozen on the wall.

"Reverend Blakeman says that some creatures were put on earth to help man, and some to hinder. The wolf, he says, is a hinderer."

"I'd rather meet the slanted eyes of a pack of rabid wolves than have a single Red Man set his heart on my scalp."

"The Reverend says—"

"The Reverend wouldn't last an hour beyond the gate of the palisade. He'd eat poison ivy or step on a rattler. The Reverend fights the wilderness with words." Pervis plucked another sticky burr from his knee-stocking and tossed it softly into the fire. "No matter. There be shillings in the till."

The yellow flames leaped again.

"And how long, sir, would a *woman* last?"

Pervis seemed caught on the thought of his shillings. "Woman?"

"Beyond the gate of the palisade. Would she step on a snake?"

Pervis neither laughed nor smiled, but dug out another burr and rolled it in his fingers. "Tommy Stanton says ye done alright once. But the wild is no place for a woman." The burr flew into the fire. "She slows a man down."

"Could a woman survive out there without a man, sir?"

"Alone? Out there?" Pervis nodded through the stone chimney to where the palisade ended. "Don't press yer luck."

"But I would learn, sir."

"Not from Pervis. Not from Pervis."

The wolf man spoke as if to end the conversation, but there was a dissatisfied glint in Ruth's eye. She gestured to the corner of the cabin. "My mother, sir, will not live forever."

Pervis put his palms to the fire, as if to stay Ruth's words. "A woman wants a child. A child becomes a hostage. I have learned that the hardest way. The hardest way."

The fire cracked and the flames leaped again, illuminating a face red with anguish, eyes like beads, cheeks suddenly drawn in.

"And won't ye tell me?" Ruth asked softly. "I would learn all that I can."

"It drove me to the woods forever."

Ruth's eyes gleamed. "But what happened, sir?"

"It were easier to live with wolves than with a woman."

"But—"

A thick log, narrowed through the middle like an hourglass, gave way to the flames and dropped in the fireplace, sending up a shower of sparks. Ruth stood to get the poker, and when she turned again, Pervis was on his way to the loft.

The bounty hunt continued. When the carcasses of the wolves had filled the rear wall, Pervis turned the corner of the cabin and hung them along the south side. The settlers could now follow his progress from a distance, without disturbing the Widow Paine.

Whenever a wolf was caught, Pervis reset the trap, the ground saturated with inviting natural scent. The savage instruments did their job, the metal jaws snapping shut from taut springs.

Ruth tried to imagine the agony of the wolf in the trap. Startled by the snap of metal teeth, the animal would bolt away, only to be flung back by the force of the staked chain. It would roll, leap, and snarl. Again and again it would lunge to free itself, then collapse, panting and exhausted. Moments later it would leap again, testing the will of the chain, its snagged leg bloody and numb. Finally, it would roll over and writhe in the leaves.

One morning Pervis found only the remains of a hind leg in his trap—a grisly bone, sticky with blood and fur. The wolf had chewed its way to freedom, only to die in the brush nearby. The other wolves had ravaged the carcass beyond recognition, making it difficult for Pervis to claim his ten shillings.

"The Red Man uses the snare," he told Ruth. "When sprung, the bent trees fly erect and prey hangs in midair, away from scavengers. But these wolves are too heavy, and I lack the Red Man's touch."

Nonetheless, in the rare moments when he wasn't resetting his traps or dragging carcasses home by the tail, he fiddled with slim birch trees and strips of rawhide, trying to manufacture a snare that would hold a wolf aloft.

By mid-December wolves hung stiff on all four walls of the cabin and Pervis began to string them along the palisade. The settlers came to gape at the bedraggled frozen carcasses, talking in low tones of the savage creatures the Lord had created.

Whenever another wolf was bound at the hind legs and draped from a peg, Ruth stood before the ragged carcass and called it friend. *Mogke-oaas*, the great animal. At times she could taste in her mouth the wolf flesh she had eaten years ago.

One afternoon, as she stood in silence before the carcass of a rust-red wolf, Mr. Bassett stepped up behind her. She jumped.

"Didn't mean to startle!" the schoolmaster chimed. "I've just dismissed the children for the day. How goes the count?" His long black coat hid his swallow-tail suit.

Ruth didn't answer, her hand spread before her throat, on the coarse material of her cloak.

Mr. Bassett reached out and stroked the tail of the carcass.

"Don't!" Ruth warned suddenly. "There— It could be rabid, could it not?"

"Indeed." Mr. Bassett withdrew his hand. "Tell me, Venus, does Mr. Pervis count his shillings at night? Is it true he neither eats nor sleeps?"

Ruth's cloak flew out at the elbows, her hands on her hips. "But for the unkindness of thy students, Mr. Bassett, the man would be lodging somewhere else."

"Indeed, indeed." The schoolmaster turned his gaze to the palisade. Several dozen carcasses hung at even intervals in the growing shadows. "A prisoner of greed, Ruth. Our Mr. Pervis is a prisoner of greed!"

"He was sent for, was he not? By advertisement. Mr. Pervis only answers Stratford's call. What would ye have him do, turn and leave?"

"The trouble," the schoolmaster said, his finger beating the air, "be not with what he does but how he does it!"

"From the looks of things, sir, most effectively."

"With a delight both loathesome and dark!"

Ruth smiled. "Why, sir. He is as efficient at his calling as you. Only he prefers wolves to students. Or to women."

"The man profits," Mr. Bassett blustered, "from our adversity!"

"And adversity, according to our good Reverend, cleanses the heart and purifies the mind. Have ye not heard our Reverend's sermon on adversity?"

Charles Bassett shook his head gravely, the swallow tails of his coat hanging dejectedly. "Take that sermon to thy heart," he said finally, "and may adversity purify thine own ideas."

Ruth looked away abruptly. Reverend Blakeman had appeared with his family on the parade grounds, leading them across to the palisade in single file. Despite the protests of his wife, he led his family daily to view the wolves, as an example for the others to follow.

John Blakeman marched behind his mother in his best trainband step, then came his brothers and sisters in order of age—Mary, James, Samuel, Deliverance, and Benjamin. The youngest Blakeman was now twelve years old.

Ruth took advantage of their arrival to slip away, leaving Mr. Bassett with his finger in the air.

18.

A Christmas Surprise

TWICE a week Pervis went off with Moses Wheeler, only to return after midnight roaring drunk. Rumor held that they met at the arsenal beneath the Watchhouse at the northern gate, where their revels would offend the fewest people.

Jane Blakeman was vehement. "My big brother," she complained to Goody Thomson, "hath little sense. I fear lest he one day tumble from his ferry and drown himself!"

Goody Thomson patted her hands on her growing womb. " 'Be not drunk with wine, wherein there is excess; but be filled with the spirit.' As for me, I pray that Mr. Pervis will be gone before my time is come."

Reverend Blakeman was silent on the matter. He didn't want to offend Mr. Pervis. The wolf man was essential to Stratford's salvation.

The weather continued clear and cold, without snow. Then one morning, less than two weeks before Christmas, Pervis woke to find his traps empty. The pits were empty too, and during the night, two sows had been slain in their pens.

He took his leather bag and sprinkled the traps and pits with wolf scent, carefully covering his tracks. But in the morning his devices were empty once again, and the wolves had killed three sheep in the paddock outside the postern gate.

Pervis ordered torches set along the palisade.

"Wise to their own scent!" he said to Ruth. "Time to fish!"

Disappearing for several days, he sought out the streams and brooks that fed the Pootatuck. When he returned, his burlap sack bulged with catfish, eels, and carp. Thomas Uffoot, at the new mill, agreed to grind a bushel of the catch, but he refused to help any further. The stench was offending the customers who came for their sacks of grain.

Pervis borrowed a sausage grinder and finished the job by hand in front of the fire while Widow Paine slept. Filling a barrel, he let the oily mash sit for three days, the heat of the flames helping the fish to decompose. In summer a cloth screen would have been necessary to prevent flies from depositing their eggs, but in winter there was no such need.

Widow Paine waved her broom wildly. She had grown used to the pungent wolf scent, but what was this? She flung the front door wide open.

The oily stink spread about the home-lots, provoking nausea. The settlers went straight to Reverend Blakeman.

"Enough!" Thomas Hawley argued. "How many wolves must be killed?"

"My wife," said Jon Thomson, "is with child. The foul odor keeps her abed. Surely there must be other baits and scents!"

Reverend Blakeman shrugged his shoulders and furled his brow.

That night, when the torches along the palisade had burned low, a small band of wolves leaped the paddock outside the northern gate and slaughtered several cows before the ruckus was discovered. Sergeant Nichols came running with the sentries and drove the wolves away with musket fire. Two were slain, but two cows were also hit. Five cows lost in one quick raid.

In the morning, the settlers gathered at the paddock to survey the carnage.

Pervis kept to his loft until Reverend Blakeman knocked on

the cabin door, a long woolen scarf pressed to his nose.

The wolf man tugged his red knit cap about his ears. "My services end here," he said quietly, "unless fish be used."

"Use what ye must, ye have my blessing!" the Reverend answered quickly. He waved a hand in front of his face and coughed into his scarf. "I have instructed all to pray for the return of winter winds—to blow this foul stench to Sewenhacky!"

Pervis went straight to work, spreading the fish scent about the traps and pits. The next morning he dragged back eight frozen carcasses and promptly hung them within the palisade. The pens and paddocks were unmolested.

"The man works miracles!" Reverend Blakeman exulted. "He keeps the very Devil at bay in the face of Christmas!"

Jane Blakeman towered above her husband. "And makes a drunkard of my brother to boot!"

Light flurries swirled up the Pootatuck on Christmas morning, but the snow refused to accumulate. The settlers huddled warmly in the Meeting House.

Pervis was not present, nor had he attended a single Sabbath service. His absence was excused by Reverend Blakeman. "He makes a contribution to the building of God's great kingdom. Thou shalt not be afraid of terror by night!"

Then, with the customary announcements, came a surprise. Sergeant Nichols was to marry Anne Wines.

"*Who?*" Seated in the very last bench, Anna Paine spoke up loudly, her hearing failing.

"*Don't know!*" Ruth whispered. "*One of the new ones!*"

The congregation buzzed, swords and muskets rattling.

"The Sergeant hath long been married to his train-band," the Reverend continued in a joyous tone, "but now he retires to home and hearth! Mine own son John inherits command of our militia!"

Ruth was shocked. For ten long years she had consciously

avoided Francis Nichols, stung by the vicious rumors that had followed the loss of his wife and her own return from the forest. The Sergeant, too, had made a habit of keeping to himself. Their mutual silence had grown into an unspoken understanding, a source of strength that came from mutual oppression. They both had suffered unjustly at the hands of the community, and yet they had remained—or so Ruth thought— unyielding and alone.

But now Sergeant Nichols was to marry. Where did that leave *her?* She was filled with disbelief.

Not once in ten years had Sergeant Nichols been seen in the company of a woman and suddenly, he was engaged to Anne Wines!

The handsome Sergeant beamed proudly in his seat.

Sitting among the women directly across the aisle from him, the pretty Anne Wines blushed beneath her white cap, a thick shawl wrapped about her thin shoulders. She was certainly attractive enough, Ruth noticed, but of the same constitution as Mary Nichols before her. Whence, she wondered, came the Sergeant's preference for such frail companionship?

Goody Blakeman twisted in her seat and looked to the hindmost rows, confused. How could she have missed such a piece of news!

Ruth's thoughts spun in her head. She heard neither the sermon nor the Psalms, her lips moving mechanically as Deacon Wells led the singing. She felt abandoned. What could have made Sergeant Nichols suddenly give up his solitary way of life and decide to marry again? She was sure it was not love. She wasn't jealous, just deeply disappointed.

And John Blakeman to command the train-band! He had always considered himself commander anyway, shouting his drill instructions across the parade grounds louder than necessary. He had too much of his mother in him, too much the boss. And his father had always encouraged him to lead.

Dressed in his iron hat and breastplate for Christmas, John

Blakeman looked about pompously from the middle of the front row.

At midday, wrapped in mufflers and cloaks, the settlers hurried through the snow flurries to their waiting meals.

Sergeant Nichols fought his way through a crowd of well-wishers on the riverbank, the young Anne Wines on his arm.

Ducking out from his lodging at the rear of the Meeting House, Charles Bassett intercepted Ruth and Anna Paine as they crossed by the stocks and whipping post.

"O, sing, sweetness, to the last palpitation of the evening and the breeze!"

Anna Paine gave the schoolmaster a dour look, then turned to Ruth. She had never seen Mr. Bassett before, nor had Ruth ever bothered to mention him. Lowering her chin, the Widow trudged on ahead into the blowing wind.

"Marriage banns mean wedding bells! What think'st thou of our brave Sergeant?"

Ruth slowed her pace out of courtesy, but the thought of Sergeant Nichols and Anne Wines left her speechless.

"What? No reply? Art thou a Stoic, Venus, in matters of the heart?"

The funny word made Ruth smile. "A *what*, sir?"

"A *Stoic*. Hast thou not read Epictetus?"

Ruth halted and stared briefly at the frosty grass, then pointed ahead toward the parade grounds, to the broad back of Anna Paine. "Nay, sir. I have no time for reading. I must spend my time with my mother."

"And I must spend Christmas alone."

"Alone, sir?"

The schoolmaster nodded eagerly, his sandy locks tossed by the wind. "Alone. No invitation."

" 'Twere an oversight, most certainly."

"Then let me extend the hospitality to thy mother and thee: Christmas dinner in my poor humble digs. A wingèd bird plucked and roasted to perfection, basted with a gravy of mine own."

Ruth smiled at the thought, unable to imagine the odd threesome in the annex of the Meeting House. Then she shook her head briskly. Anna Paine was a hundred yards ahead. "Nay, sir. It would take such considerable explaining, and my mother understands less and less. She is comfortable the most at home. But in the spirit of the season, sir, I thank thee. Happy Christmas, Mr. Bassett."

"Happy Christmas, then." The schoolmaster bowed politely and turned away.

Ruth hurried off, afraid to look back, afraid of the ruddy cheeks and hazel eyes. Why should she suddenly feel so guilty? Were it not enough to care for Widow Paine?

As she cut through the pines at the corner of the Blakeman home-lot, the Reverend's wife stepped out on the front porch and shouted, loud enough for all of Stratford to hear, " 'A violent man enticeth his neighbor and leadeth him into the way that is not good!' "

Moses Wheeler had just entered the Reverend's house for Christmas dinner. The "violent man," Ruth guessed, was Pervis. But were the words meant for Moses Wheeler or herself?

The burly ferry keeper waved brightly from behind a glass window, clowning at his sister's expense, and Ruth suddenly began to run, her laughter clouded with tears.

Unable to sleep, Ruth listened fearfully as Pervis and Moses Wheeler returned to the cabin late at night.

"Jolly Christmas, Fish-worth! Thine own stink be worse than thy bait!"

"Bye and bye, oaf! Bye and bye!"

The big man was too drunk to lift his companion into the loft. He deposited him within the door and wandered away, groping in the darkness like a blind man.

Pervis crawled to the fire. Ruth had added a supply of logs earlier, but they had burned low.

The shallow wooden tub by the nail keg was full of cold water. Pervis knelt and dunked his head right in, knit cap and all. He came up hatless, his buckskin jacket soaked to the elbow.

Flinging a few logs in the direction of the dying flames, he poured the water into the large black kettle hanging in the fireplace. Then, while Ruth watched, he stripped off his clothes, hopping in place in an effort to warm himself.

Oh, wicked nakedness!

And yet Ruth watched, intrigued by the strange man's body. Were I a man, she thought, my body would be similar, for I have never been more than a slender swamp reed.

Even the reddish hair is similar. It would be thick and curly across his scalp were it not for the scar.

Ruth thought of the wolf man trapping in the north. Here was a man who, unlike Thomas Stanton, feared the Red Man more than the wolves.

And she herself feared neither.

Not even God.

The blasphemous realization had come to her that morning, despite Reverend Blakeman's sermon. No God would make Francis Nichols up and marry, without reason, without time. No God would make a good woman like Anna Paine live as a widow, or make Pervis wander the woods alone. And if there were a Divine Plan, as the Reverend proclaimed, it certainly did not include her.

She couldn't prove it, she just knew it in her bones.

Not that she cared. She knew only that she was warm beneath her rust-red wolf pelt, that she had been to the woods once and returned unharmed. That she could do it again if she had to.

And no longer, she realized on this cold, dark Christmas night, was she ashamed by the sight of the wolf man's body.

19.

The Windsor Witch

THE small joys of Christmas ended abruptly. A traveler cross-
ing the Pootatuck on Moses Wheeler's ferry brought word that
a witch had been discovered in Windsor.

The Devil had appeared to the old woman in the guise of a
bird. Confessing her sin after repeated questioning, she was
promptly hung from the tallest oak in the settlement.

The Stratfordites were stunned. Certainly witches had been
discovered in Europe. The settlers had heard tales of fear and
terror since departing. But in the New World? In Connecticut?

"And if in Windsor," Reverend Blakeman said quietly, "then
anywhere." He retreated to his study and surrounded himself
with his books, announcing a Lecture Day.

Talk of wolves halted immediately, and so did talk of Pervis, Moses Wheeler, Sergeant Nichols and Anne Wines. One
thought troubled all: a witch discovered in Windsor!

Ruth couldn't imagine such goings-on. She had known but a
handful of families at the trading post, all of them common-
sense people. But Windsor had grown since she had left there
with Anna Paine to join Reverend Blakeman's band in Sandy
Hollow. What changes had ten years brought?

"Know ye," the Reverend began on Lecture Day, "that there
are devils and witches, and that those night-birds do not appear
where there is the daylight of the gospel. And yet our New
England has examples of their existence and operations: not
only in the wigwams of the Red Man, where the pagan pow-

wows often raise their masters in the shapes of snakes, bears, or wolves: but in the House of Christians, where our God has had his constant worship. These have undergone annoyance of evil spirits. We must pray for our brethren in Windsor, for they have acted upon God's word.

"As we read in Exodus, 'Thou shalt not suffer a witch to live.' And again in our Colonial Code, 'If any man or woman be a witch, they shall be put to death.' "

The Reverend grasped the front of the pulpit with both hands, but his tone, unlike the previous Lecture Day, was cautious, inquisitive, probing.

"It remains for our brethren in Windsor to consider what evils hath provoked the Lord to bring His judgment unto them, and what must be done so these evils may be reformed."

Although the Reverend spoke of Windsor, there was not a member of the congregation huddled in the Meeting House who did not think of Stratford. And such was the Reverend's intent.

"True religion," the Reverend continued, "consists of the holy worship of God. To advance this worship, the rooting out of witches and witchcraft is a special service and acceptable duty unto God. We are commanded to do so, not only in Exodus but in Leviticus, Matthew, and Deuteronomy. However, even among learned men there is much disagreement and contradiction on the subject of witchcraft. From the outpouring of general ignorance and superstitious blindness, I will try to declare what portion of certainty God and nature hath defined and allowed. If I err, my brethren, be not ashamed to acknowledge thy better knowledge. The truth shall be our judge."

It was warm in the Meeting House, the huge fireplace blazing. On the bench in the very last row, Anna Paine began to snore. Her chin dropped to her chest and she leaned against Ruth.

The white sands of Ipswich fell through the brassbound hourglass, faster than the recent snow flurries. Ruth poked the widow and pushed her erect.

"It remains to ask about witchcraft," the Reverend explained, "whether it is in the common way of detection of all truths, or by itself has privileges beyond all other trials."

The following morning, as if to continue his lecture, Reverend Blakeman ordered Moses Wheeler into the stocks until sunset. A Bible was propped on a barrel in front of him, opened to Proverbs, Chapter 23, and the big man spent the day repeating aloud: " 'Who hath woe? Who hath sorrow? Who hath contentions? Who hath babbling? Who hath wounds without cause? Who hath redness of the eyes? They that tarry long at the wine!' "

The action, undertaken upon the advice of Nicolas Knell, was rumored to have been urged by Jane Blakeman herself. Nonetheless, the message was clear. As Goody Thomson told her husband, "Resist the Devil and he will flee from thee. Satan is at work in those who are disobedient. Stratford is not Windsor—the Reverend will see to it!"

On their way to and from the Meeting House, the children taunted the ferry keeper, reciting along with him as if in Mr. Bassett's classroom: "Who hath woe! Who hath sorrow!"

The burly man knelt in the cold mud, head and wrists locked within stiff oak planks. Only Ruth was not cruel, wiping his face and bringing him water to drink while the settlers took their midday meal.

Returning toward dark, Pervis crossed the parade grounds to investigate the unexpected crowd near the Meeting House. He reeked of dead fish. But what was this? Moses Wheeler?

The big man had just been released and was standing bent, rubbing his neck.

Pervis laughed, calling from a distance in a rusty voice. "Take stock of thyself, oaf! Take *stock*!"

His remark was the last bit of humor the settlers were to enjoy for months to come.

On the Sabbath, Reverend Blakeman announced that the

Lecture Days would continue until all areas of witchcraft had been explored.

"Mr. Pervis keeps the Devil without the gate," he reminded the congregation. "It falls to me to keep him from within. 'Yea woe is unto me, if I preach not the gospel!' Thus we read in First Corinthians."

The new year came in clear and cold. In the absence of snow the settlers worked busily, piling cords of wood about the home-lots. Stiff offshore winds blew the fish stench away, and the scent continued to fool the wolves. Frozen carcasses, bound at the hind legs, hung from pegs for nearly one hundred yards along the palisade.

"It is a hard and difficult matter to detect witchcraft by the ordinary courses," Reverend Blakeman began on the next Lecture Day. "For if God had allowed men to always satisfy their intentions and desires, without failing, what would become of religion, virtue, and wisdom? Men would become so confident in their own strengths and power, and so proud, that they would forget God. Therefore Almighty God, in his great and unspeakable wisdom, hath subjected vain man, thereby to teach him wisdom, piety, trust, dependence, worship, and adoration.

"Since God and nature hath limited the powers of scrutiny of man, unto what other bar or seat of justice can witchcraft appeal or be brought? It may be objected, the art of witchcraft being supernatural and the practice thereof sustained by an extraordinary power, that therefore the means and ways of discovery must be likewise more than ordinary and supernatural. Hereto is truly answered, that since the nature and power of spirits is unknown to man, and is not known otherwise, but by examining the works issuing from thence, and by comparing them aright with that which is natural, therefore the works of the Devil and witches, though sustained and produced by a supernatural power, yet hath no other way for their detection by man, but that which is ordinary to man and natural and possible to man.

"And therefore let men be persuaded and contented in this only warranted way to patiently seek the true discovery, to find the footing, the path, and the steppings of witchcraft, as of all other things."

Following the lecture, the settlers huddled and grumbled outside on the riverbank.

"Good God Gravy," Moses Wheeler complained. "If the Devil be among us, he will surely flee the Meeting House! It were easier to spend the day in yon stocks!"

"Nay," warned Nicolas Knell. "Did not the Reverend speak of patience?"

"So he did," agreed the schoolmaster. "He proceedeth as he must, with thorough caution."

Ruth had not attended the lecture. Given the seriousness of the subject, she feared the widow's snoring might distract the listeners. She spent the day mending the ragged holes in the wolf man's knee-stockings.

And at night she watched him bathe.

20.

The Dutchman

BY the middle of January, the wolves had grown wise to the fish scent. Pervis had known all along that they would, but he was disturbed that they had caught on so quickly.

The moment he found his traps empty, he promptly hiked out the path to the ferry.

"Find me a Dutchman, oaf. Any Dutchman passin' 'twixt here and Manhattas. I have ten shillings for every Dutchman found!"

Moses Wheeler nodded abruptly and Pervis went on his way.

Back at the cabin, he placed fifty shillings on the nail keg in five gleaming stacks and informed Anna Paine that he now owned her entire stock of tallow.

The old woman resisted.

"I've no time to argue," Pervis declared.

Ruth immediately escorted the widow out the door for a walk about the palisade.

Left alone to his work, Pervis took a fishhook and rolled it into a ball of waxy tallow. He made several dozen such balls, each no larger than a small, hard apple.

When the supply of fishhooks was exhausted, he inserted sharp pieces of bone. And when the tallow was gone, he rolled the bones into fresh animal fat. Having filled the burlap sack, he headed into the woods to scatter the balls about the scent posts.

The yellow substance would melt quickly when the wolves

ate them, and the bones and fishhooks cause a slow death from internal bleeding.

Pervis continued to drag home the ragged carcasses and hang them within the palisade. The settlers were relieved that the fish stench was gone for good.

One January afternoon, while Anna Paine slept, Ruth wandered off in the general direction Pervis had taken that morning. It was too cold to ride the ferry. Wrapped in her cloak, she walked briskly over the frozen ground, her mind on the strange man who preferred wolves to women. At the far edge of the New Field she entered the woods, kicking through the dry leaves.

For fear of wolves the settlers generally avoided the woods, but Pervis had assured her it was safe by light of day.

The sun shone brightly overhead, showing the way between the leafless trees. The paths were many, the underbrush no longer the tangle it was in the bloom of summer. White birches stood out among the green pines and the purple trunks of maple and oak.

Feeling lighter with every step away from the palisade, Ruth ventured deeper into the woods than ever before, half hoping to encounter the dark eyes she had seen through the years. Those dark, watchful eyes had disappeared with the arrival of Pervis. She wondered if she would ever seen them again. Had they really been there? It seemed unlikely she could conjure them at will.

Eventually, stepping across a sunken brook, she found herself in a small clearing bound on the west side by a long granite ledge. The ledge was just high enough to sit on, wide enough to provide a partial shelter for the clearing. Beyond the ledge, a tall oak rose straight up into the sky, sending a wide branch, like a sturdy protective arm, overhead. A fat gray squirrel crouched precariously on the very end of the limb, an acorn fixed in its paws.

Ruth stood and stared at the face of the granite ledge. It was streaked horizontally with layers of gray and white. Originally it must have been a shelflike boulder; now only half remained. The granite appeared to have been systematically heated, then split and hauled away.

On his return from treating with the Pequannocks, Captain Mason had told of granite pillars. They were arranged in a wide circle around which the Red Man danced, making strange gestures and singing strange songs. The agreement signed, Captain Mason had been invited to watch. The dances, as Queriheag made clear, ensured fertility, the growth and continued life of all good things.

Captain Mason had described them as heathen ritual, as one more reason to put the Red Man in his place until the word of Christ could sink in.

Ruth wondered about the christening of Nimrod. Had he truly accepted the White Man's God at the close of the Pequot War? Or had he simply acted in self-defense, to save himself from the forces of Captain Mason?

Something splashed noisily in the sunken brook above the clearing.

"Mr. Pervis?"

Ruth's voice was almost fearful. Pervis, she knew, walked the woods as silently as the Red Man.

Then she saw a huge wolf, a ragged gray, crashing along with spastic movements, head twitching from side to side. With every other step it stopped abruptly as if to drink, then shook its head wildly and splashed on, lashing out in all directions.

Ruth stiffened, pressing back against the ledge. It was the first wolf she had seen alive since Nimrod's burnt offering was dragged from the clearing that strange night long ago.

The gray's scraggly mane bristled as it whipped its head from side to side, snapping and snarling. Then suddenly it quieted, slinking along for a few yards, only to explode from the brook in a rage, twisting and whining in the leaves.

The thick pads of its feet, normally tougher than leather, were badly cut, its thick fur knotted with burrs. Rolling over, it leaped erect, black lips white with froth. Seeing Ruth, it stopped and snapped its jaws.

Ruth's hands flew into the air, and for a brief moment her eyes met the wolf's. The wolf stood absolutely still. Then an acorn hit the leaves at the edge of the clearing, and the large animal leaped away unnaturally.

Writhing along the shallow bank, it rooted in the leaves like a pig, finally bounding off through the trees in jerky flight.

"It weren't the tallow," Pervis said later. "When a thirsty wolf can't drink, it's rabies. There's nothin' meaner. Yer a lucky woman." He tugged his red knit cap about his ears. "Keep it under yer hat."

In the morning Moses Wheeler sent a Dutchman up from the ferry. Pervis was hanging a carcass on the palisade. The two men talked briefly, then the Dutchman went on his way.

"No good," Pervis said, handing the ferry keeper ten shillings. The fringe of his buckskin jacket flapped in a stiff breeze. "Find me another. Any Dutchman passin' 'twixt here and Manhattas."

Moses Wheeler nodded, and Pervis stalked off to check his pits.

The following morning, Reverend Blakeman continued his lecture on witchcraft.

"All knowledge that goes beyond the knowledge of man must come from the knowledge of spirits. But how shall the works of *good* spirits be known and distinguished from the works of devils?

"All the works of good spirits are observed to be, like the spirits themselves, holy, good, and freely serving the will of Almighty God. All works that come from spirits that cannot be proved to be first commanded by God, or tending solely to the execution of His will, are certainly to be suspected as works of devils. God doth permit—as we read in the third book of Saint Augustine—such works, partly to deceive the wicked, and partly to quicken the godly and holy man, to prove him thereby, as He did his faithful and obedient servant Job.

"It is not the supernatural work itself but the contract and combination with the Devil, the consent and allowance thereof, that doth make a witch. It remains to consider how these supernatural works may be detected.

"Many such works of the Devil are visible to us. Did not the Devil, in the body of a serpent, miraculously speak with Eve, as we read in Genesis? Was not this speech truly heard? Was not the fire brought down from Heaven in so miraculous a manner, and in so extraordinary a power, to destroy so many thousands of Job's sheep? Was not this truly visible?

"These supernatural works of the Devil are not apparitions or illusions, but are visible to us. And these works are likewise evident to Reason.

"That we may build the foundation of Reason upon the truth of God's holy word, let us for the detection of witches seek out God's word and draw our conclusions."

Following the lecture, Charles Bassett found Ruth walking Anna Paine across the parade grounds. "Thine absence at the Meeting House," he said quietly, "goes not unnoticed."

"I tend to my mother, sir. You see her present distraction. She fares not well, as the Reverend knows."

The widow kept her eyes to the ground, her thick chin tucked to her broad chest.

"The Reverend speaks frequently of knowledge."

"But that is not my province, sir."

"When one meets the world with a sound education, there be no turning aside from wild beasts."

Ruth cocked her head. "Do ye mean wolves, sir?"

"Aye, Ruth; wolves of all sorts."

Ruth frowned, her cloak flying wide at the elbows as her hands went to her hips. "Not *all* wolves need be feared, sir."

The schoolmaster blew a steamy breath into the woolen muffler about his neck. "What news of our pestilent Pervis?"

"Will ye never speak well of the man? Mr. Pervis harbors a dark and private sorrow, something long ago that sent him to a life in the woods. He hath hinted of it often but will not speak on it directly, though I have tried, sir, to draw him out."

"I would not seek the knowledge of such a sorrow for all the balm in Gilead."

"What? A man of learning who fears to know?"

"Not all knowledge is sacred, Ruth."

"And yet I would learn, sir—"

"Heed thy Reverend!"

"—and know all."

At the end of the week, Sergeant Nichols was wedded to the young Anne Wines. According to Puritan tradition the civil ceremony was conducted by William Beardsley, current magistrate to the General Court in Hartford.

Although invited to the brief celebration, Pervis spent the day huddled in the arsenal beneath the Watchhouse, talking at length with the Dutchman he had been seeking.

21.

Snow and Silence

RUTH was not invited to the marriage of Francis Nichols. Ever since the engagement had been announced, she had cast nothing but dour looks in his direction.

Increasingly, she sensed herself alone. Anna Paine provided physical company only. Even Moses Wheeler seemed distant, as if he feared that any familiarity with her would link his name, eventually, to Pervis once again.

Marching with his men about the parade ground in endless military drill, John Blakeman had become totally aloof. And yet, whenever Ruth passed by, she felt his strong blue eyes upon her. The Reverend's son, she thought, seems confused by his own haughtiness.

But the deepest sense of loneliness stemmed from Pervis himself. What manner of man was this? What had driven him to the woods so long ago? His methodical pursuit of the wolves bordered on madness. Yet it kept him busy, and kept his mind off . . . what?

Ruth could prove nothing. She simply felt certain that Mr. Pervis was interested in more than his wolves.

Only Mr. Bassett remained openly kind, though in a bothersome way. Unlike the Reverend, he was uncommonly tolerant, his knowledge like branches extending in many directions. In contrast, the Reverend's knowledge was like the trunk of a tree.

What, then, did that make her own? Leaves that floated in the breeze, like lost feathers.

• • •

In February, the snows came in earnest, as if to make up for having delayed so long. High winds swept across from Sewenhacky, driving drifts to the very top of the palisade. The few brown leaves that rattled in the trees were stripped away and quickly buried.

Rolling whitecaps seemed to extend the snow across the Pootatuck and the Sound itself. Shuttered against the wind, the settlers huddled behind walls banked with sod. Gray smoke swirled from brick chimneys to disappear amidst the blinding flakes.

And when the winds stopped, the snow still came for two weeks running, through the middle of the month. The sun had all but disappeared, a faint glow in a distant gray sky.

No one ventured into the cold until dwindling wood supplies forced the issue. And even then it was only to the rear of the house, where cords of wood were stacked to the eaves.

Where it had not drifted, the snow was waist deep.

"Lo, the whited world!" Charles Bassett exclaimed from the bell tower, his wooly muffler wrapped about his face. Unable to see beyond the edge of the Meeting House roof, he quickly descended to the warmth of a blazing hearth. Despite his manic bell-ringing, his classroom remained empty for days on end.

Goody Thomson, seven months pregnant, endured her confinement cheerily. "Stratford itself be more confined than I!" she laughed, repeating the joke until Jon Thomson and his two sons prayed for spring.

Lost among the books in his study, Reverend Blakeman hammered out his lectures. The narrow room, an attic enclosure above the main stairwell, had no window, no light except for flickering candles.

Letters from Europe, which came six months apart, were disconcerting. They told of witchcraft and subsequent trials. Frantic, the minister pursued many topics: how witches receive knowledge from spirits; how wizards and imposters differ from witches; how men may by reason be satisfied concerning those who are truly bewitched; the casting of witches into water; the scratching, beating, and pinching of witches; the drawing of blood.

Braving snow up to his shoulders to come for dinner, old Nicolas Knell warned the Reverend against the strain of difficult study.

The Reverend seemed oblivious. "Is it not a thing commonly received," he replied, "that witches are ofttimes seen bodily to haunt places, fields, houses, graves in a wondrous and miraculous manner?"

The next Lecture Day would be held as soon as the trainband could dig a path to the Meeting House.

In the snow-covered cabin by the northern gate, Ruth watched Pervis at his work. Anna Paine snored in the far corner beneath her blankets.

"Thy mother hibernates," Pervis said, "like a bear."

Weak yellow light leaked from the square of oiled cloth, the window shuttered against the snow.

"What is sleep," Ruth answered softly, "if not an escape?"

The fire blazed. Pervis smiled—or winced—briefly. "True, wench, true. Many times I have longed to burn my throat with corn liquor and fall back into the deepest drift."

A pile of dried brown seeds sat in the center of the nail keg, spilled from a small leather pouch. The seeds were shaped like disks, an inch in diameter, a quarter inch thick. Pervis was wearing cowhide gloves.

His back to the fire, he knelt before the nail keg, a stone pestle in hand. Ever so carefully he began to grind the seeds, the brittle husks crushing readily to emit a powdery white substance.

"And do ye turn now to baking, Mr. Pervis?"

Ruth was amazed at her own willingness to talk. Normally the cabin was devoid of conversation, but now she found herself overly cautious, and the subtle tension resolved itself in speech.

There was another factor, too. For weeks Pervis had never addressed her directly, had never addressed anyone directly, averting his eyes as if to talk to himself. But now it seemed as though his deep-set eyes were fixed squarely on her own, in search of a responsive gaze.

Perhaps, Ruth thought, he had always looked directly at her. Perhaps it was the person addressed who had turned away, made uncomfortable by those deep-set eyes.

"If the Reverend baked his communion bread with *nux vomica*, his congregation would meet a savage death."

Ruth sat poised on the edge of her bed, the rust-red wolf pelt in her lap. She wore no bonnet, her long red hair a lively tangle of curls across her back. The sharp features of her face seemed chiseled from ivory.

"I have heard of no such flour, sir."

Pervis tugged his red knit cap about his ears. Purple veins strained at the surface of his ruddy cheeks. "A product of New Holland, wench, brought 'round the Cape of Good Hope by Dutch explorers, then shipped from Amsterdam to Manhattas. Dirk Hartog found it first, and his sailors paid dearly. The aborigines of New Holland make of it a poison for their arrows."

"Poison?"

More seeds spilled from the leather pouch. "The tallow lies buried," Pervis said. "By the time the snow melts, the wolves will be wise. In the meantime they starve; it's feast or famine for a wolf. The packs will return to the Reverend's livestock. There's no chance for penned creatures in fragile lean-to's."

The stone pestle rose and fell deftly, the white powder mounting in the center of the nail keg. "But at the scent posts," Pervis said suddenly, "there'll be rabbits waitin', flayed and quartered and spiced with *nux vomica*."

Ruth looked to the fire to avoid the wolf man's stare. His rusty voice grew louder.

"Mr. Blakeman will have his wolves. Each new carcass delights him terribly. He sees his fears eliminated one by one and pinned to the palisade. But the wolves, wench, be not the guilty ones."

The snow continued, the wind returning to drive it hard about the home-lots. Each morning Pervis left the palisade by the northern gate, stepping over the white surface on sinewy snowshoes.

From his smallest traps he brought home a string of hares. Skinned and split into quarters, their carcasses were sprinkled with the Dutchman's powder and set about in the woods.

The wolves reacted as Pervis knew they must. Bolting the ragged flesh crazily, they soon raged in dying fits, rolling with cramps and vomiting violently.

He let the stiffening corpses lie. Retaining the poison, the sickly meat killed the wolves that gathered in turn to feed on their ravaged brothers.

All howling soon ceased in the night, and yet, as it was readily apparent, the wolves were no longer on the move. The pens and paddocks went untouched, the livestock huddled warmly in the muddy snow and manure.

Only the Lecture Days broke the round of snow and silence. And broke it sharply. "Be not deceived by the purity of driven snow," the Reverend warned, "for witch-storms fly our way from Europe!"

Talk of Ruth's absence from the Meeting House increased, then ended abruptly when it was rumored that the widow was ill. "Let hearts be charitable," Goody Blakeman urged. "Let us remember the sacrifice of Jonas Paine."

Pervis retired to his loft to sleep and wait. "Spring's the time for a final drive," he told Ruth. "The Dutchman spoke of a ship with Irish wolfhounds, more swift and fierce than any mastiff.

Ye twist the leg of a young pig and its squealin' brings the wolves from their dens. The hounds keep 'em busy while ye drag out the pups."

Ruth lowered her eyes in the face of the deep-set stare.

"Then the wolf man will be on his way."

Finally, after days without sun, the snow stopped falling and the sun returned. It was simply there one silent morning— as silent as the Red Man, as silent as the wolves themselves. The settlers greeted it quietly within their homes, dreaming of spring.

22.

Joan of Arc

IN spite of the rumors, Anna Paine was not physically ill. She did, however, require enormous amounts of sleep, her broad, squat body tiring easily. As Pervis had observed, she seemed content to hibernate.

At times, tossing off her heap of blankets, she would rise quickly and brandish her broom about the cabin, intent on the task as it if were crucial to something she could no longer remember. Bright and clear when she awoke, her eyes would soon glaze over, like the windows in the Reverend's fine frame house. More often than not, she would drop her broom and return to bed.

She rarely spoke, and yet she seemed satisfied. Somewhere in a corner of her mind lingered the thought that Ruth had once gone away. But she also held the knowledge that Ruth had returned, that things were all right. She would be provided for. Such thoughts were enough. There was a warm fire and adequate food; these were sound stores for anyone's old age.

Pervis ignored the old woman and she ignored him, at times doubting that he was really there. At night Ruth sometimes found her sitting upright in the bed across the way, gray hair hanging from her nightcap like strings, staring at the square opening to the loft.

What was she thinking? That an angular man in a red knit cap had just leaped up there from the nail keg? Or that in the

152

cold pine-scented trunks beyond the beams lay the personal effects of Jonas Paine?

Dear, dear Jonas. He had gone off from Windsor to . . . what?
To fight the Pequots. Aye. But unlike Ruth, he had never returned. So long ago, so long ago.

Time was such a fuzzy animal. Better to sleep and beat the air
with a broom.

Ruth loved the silent days of sun and snow. There was time
to think. The sun's rays forced their way through the cabin
shutters, warming the oiled cloth with a broad yellow glow. On
such days it was difficult to feel lonely.

Pervis polished his traps by the nail keg or warmed himself
before the fire. Occasionally a smile would break across his face.
Whenever the widow got up, he would retire to the loft, where
he could be heard humming to himself. He seemed so gentle,
so content. How could anyone doubt his motives? Ruth felt
ashamed for having doubted them herself.

One morning, with Pervis and the widow still asleep, Ruth
put on the wolf's man's snowshoes. Bundled in a cloak, muffler,
and three long skirts, she clomped from the cabin for the first
time in weeks, sinking only slightly into the snow with each un-
wieldy step. Ah, what a release to be outdoors!

The clean, cold air drilled her nostrils and stung her lungs.
Every exhalation came in short puffs of steam. The world stood
still, ringed in solid blue. By the northern gate a bluejay
screeched, indignant.

Trudging awkwardly across the frozen New Field, Ruth
squinted into the glare of the snow. Reaching the woods, she
followed the sunken brook until she came to the clearing with
the long granite ledge.

The ledge lay covered with a smooth mound of snow. So,
too, she guessed, would be Nimrod's breadloaf lodge, miles farther into the woods at the Pequannock village.

And what was he doing, what was he thinking, huddled within?

A large crow flew from the tall oak beyond the clearing, showering the black branches with powdery snow. Ruth moved off as well, lost in sunshine and shadow, following the winding brook for a full hour until it emerged at the far end of the Old Field.

The salt hay waved like hair from the drifts along the bluffs. Just beyond, the Sound lay rippled and black, Sewenhacky a purple band on the horizon. Only at the water's edge was the sand free of snow.

And there, far up the shore, was the Red Man's shell heap, gleaming like a giant icicle, so perfectly solid and alone.

Kee-urr! Kee-urr! A single tern swept up the frozen beach, skirting the salt hay until it turned for the Sound.

For some reason Ruth recalled the words of Goody Thomson, something she had overheard as she had fled the Meeting House after the wedding announcement of Sergeant Nichols and Anne Wines.

"A woman in the wilderness who doesn't marry is a poor, wretched creature, the shriveled fruit of humanity, sharp and bitter to the taste, with no sweet juices."

Why, she wondered, should that be so? Why couldn't she live like Nimrod or Thomas Stanton, or even Pervis himself? Stratford was not the wilderness. The wilderness lay beyond the palisade, up the Pootatuck, at the granite ledge, along the Sound. Had she not survived there perfectly alone? And had it not been enough?

Sunlight sparkled on the iced-over shell heap, and Ruth turned for the palisade, shaken by a sudden chill.

It was late in the afternoon when she returned. Charles Bassett met her at the postern gate. The schoolmaster stood before a raging bonfire where members of the train-band were warming themselves, shovels on their shoulders like muskets.

"Fair Venus of the ruby lips and ruddy cheeks! Hast thou entered into the treasures of the snow?"

Ruth clomped wearily within the gate and leaned against the palisade in an area cleared of drifts. "Quite so, Mr. Bassett. Quite so."

"Thy energy is enviable."

"My energy is spent." Ruth hugged her elbows, shivering.

"Then step to the fire and remove thy foreign appendages. See! The way stands clear to the northern gate."

Ruth nodded, looking beyond the leaping flames of the fire. The snow lay piled head high along a narrow, frozen path that twisted its way through the home-lots to the parade grounds.

Kneeling at Ruth's feet, the schoolmaster untied the thongs, and she stepped free of the snowshoes.

"Such walking requires a hearty soul!"

Again Ruth nodded, extending her palms to the fire. Her ankles throbbed.

Mr. Bassett stood briskly. "At his latest lecture the Reverend spoke of Jean D'Arc. I was reminded of you."

"I know of no one, sir, by the name of John Dark."

The schoolmaster smiled. "Joan of Arc, Ruth. The infamous Frenchwoman."

"I know not her either."

Mr. Bassett tossed his muffler over his shoulder. "No matter. I was reminded of you."

In the silence that followed Ruth stared at her feet. The heat of the bonfire had melted the snow and turned the earth to a circle of mud.

"She bore a fiercely independent spirit," the schoolmaster said after a while, assuming his classroom voice. "Inspired by miraculous revelations, she led the French armies against the English. Then she was taken prisoner and burnt at the stake —for witchcraft. Such revelations, Reverend Blakeman insists, are ever in their proper nature solely attendant upon God. To make of them a thing of common practice must necessarily proceed from the Devil."

Ruth stepped closer to the fire. In the distance she could see Moses Wheeler wielding a shovel, heaving snow above the members of the train-band. His ferry lay buried in drifts on the bank of the Pootatuck.

"One is either a sober citizen subject to God's law, or the Devil's offspring."

"And be there," Ruth asked quietly, "no other state?"

Charles Bassett hesitated a moment, then stomped his feet for warmth. "Nay, Ruth. Not in Stratford."

The sun was sinking rapidly in the west. Ruth clapped the snowshoes together, then held them before the fire to melt the ice from the strings.

"This Joan of Arc, Mr. Bassett: what were her revelations?"

"She heard voices. The witch so lately hung in Windsor spoke to a bird. Revelations come at sundry times and in diverse manners. But as the Reverend says—"

"—they proceed from the Devil."

"It were wise to believe it."

"And were it wise to deny a bird's song?"

"That, Venus, depends on what it sings."

"And if its tail feather spells out the truth in the sand?"

"I would avoid such a bird at all costs."

"And yet I have seen it, sir, with mine own eyes."

John Blakeman strode down the narrow, snowy path, his eyes fixed on the couple by the postern gate. When he reached the bonfire he planted a heel hard in the melting snow, pivoted, and marched off again.

"*Pewsagl!*" Charles Bassett exclaimed.

"Pews haggle, sir? About what?"

"*Pewsagl.* Pride. Envy. Wrath. Sloth. Avarice. Gluttony. Lust. It were a student's way of remembering. Young Blakeman has his share of the seven deadly sins!"

Ruth nodded in agreement. "Aye, he walks as proud as his mother."

"And lusts for Stratford's Venus."

Ruth lowered her eyes. "Thou art most perceptive, sir."

"And envious!"

"Envious? Of whom, sir?"

"Why, me, Ruth. Of us." The schoolmaster spoke as if his words were common knowledge.

A sudden wind from Sewenhacky bent the flames toward the northern gate.

Ruth shivered. "I must go, sir, before I take chill." She hurried away up the narrow, snowy path. "I have tarried too long, my mother waits! Let us put such foolish talk on ice!"

Soon home, she found Anna Paine sitting on the nail keg with her broom fixed in her fat fists, her stumpy legs short of the earthen floor. A soft glaze coated her eyes.

Pervis peeked from the rafters. "Thy bear holds me prisoner, wench! In the future, please tend to thy duty!"

Setting the snowshoes aside, Ruth took the broom from the widow and led her to her bed in the corner. Then Pervis dropped from the loft and stomped from the cabin.

23.

Nux Vomica

MARCH was one long month of freezing rain, each gray day indistinguishable from the next. The wet snow shrunk to inches, the pathways rutted in slush. Twigs and branches, coated with ice, snapped from trees and fell about the home-lots. For the first time in weeks the bedraggled carcasses of the wolves were visible along the palisade. Stratford lay dormant, like a seed in the earth.

In early April the sun returned, accompanied by a brisk, warm wind. The sodden turf and thatched roofs began to dry out. The ice left the wells and ponds. In the woods, the brooks were brimming, and green shoots waited beneath dead leaves.

Then the winds died and the days grew brighter and warmer. The marsh grass thickened. A rich smell rose along the bluffs. Fresh breezes rolled up the Pootatuck, stirring the scent of hemlock and pine. The fragrance of bayberry and hawthorne drifted from the inland hills and the fields began to shine with flowers—marsh marigolds and purple phlox. The livestock grew restless for pasture.

During the harsh months, the settlers had been dreaming of England, of primrose lanes and the clatter of cobblestone. They took heart from the gray squirrels that darted about the parade grounds. Though lean from the ravages of winter, the squirrels were larger than any ever seen in Derbyshire. Now the past was put away. Time for a garden in the corner of the yard.

And then, in the spirit of the season, a baby girl arrived, named for Rebecca in the Bible.

Goody Thomson beamed, her long confinement ended. Jon Thomson and his two sons marveled at the pink and wrinkled infant, at its shrill and ceaseless crying.

Reverend Blakeman was ecstatic. His lectures had ended; the wolves were silenced. The Red Man had all but disappeared. And now a child, a new life at the end of winter's sorrow, a new soul for America's Eden!

"The children of Stratford," he exclaimed on the Sabbath, "are chosen for extraordinary work! Forget ye not God's promise to Abraham: 'Get thee out of thy country . . . unto a land that I will show thee: and I will make of thee a great nation!'"

Families came, one by one, to view the infant. Francis Nichols was first, leading his shy bride. Baby Thomson lay in a wooden cradle beside the fireplace, wrapped in sheepskin, screaming at the spring.

In the warmer weather the wolf carcasses thawed and began to rot. When the putrid odor, stronger than the fish stench, became unbearable, Pervis dragged the wolves away by the tail, two at a time, burying them in the same pits that had trapped them.

The carcasses had served their purpose. Each one had brought ten shillings in bounty, and their grisly display had pleased the Reverend no end.

And yet Pervis worried. The total inactivity of the remaining wolves puzzled him. The depleted packs existed in silence.

It could mean only one thing—something he had heard of but never witnessed, something he would know for certain soon enough when it was time to scout the wolf dens for cubs. Until then, bury the dead wolves and wait.

Ruth was relieved that Pervis was out-of-doors again, away

from the cabin. She found it increasingly difficult to avoid his deep stare. The man who had never looked squarely at anyone now seemed to look solely at *her*, his gaze at once imploring and impertinent.

At night, while he ground the seeds of *nux vomica*, she kept her face turned to the fire. Pervis, glancing up every so often from his work, broke his own concentration. He spilled the white powder about the nail keg and left it caked to the cold stone pestle.

He was distracted for a number of reasons. A party of Dutchmen ferrying the Pootatuck had brought work of a frigate lost at sea. Among its cargoes was a pack of Irish wolfhounds. A final spring drive was now impossible.

As they moved to the outlying fields for the annual planting, the settlers made a gruesome discovery. Carcasses of crows, ferrets, and skunks littered the area, and there were dozens more in the immediate woods. Had the winter been that severe?

The morning after the livestock were released from their pens, several sheep were found stiff in the frost. A spring lamb was missing. The settlers stood about, stunned.

The poisoned wolves, in the throes of death, had slobbered on the ground, and the yellow grass had retained the poison. Animals grazing about the carcasses had been stricken in turn.

"The very earth lies infected!" Thomas Uffoot cried. "What plague is this?"

Reverend Blakeman immediately counseled with Nicolas Knell, and the pair knocked on Anna Paine's door.

"Mr. Pervis has gone to the woods," Ruth explained, "seeking wolf dens."

The Reverend turned to Nicolas Knell, who shook his head, tugging on his long white beard. Then the two men hurried off across the parade grounds, into the warmest afternoon of the year. The lacy buds of Stratford's trees had burst into leaves as broad as cow's ears.

Upset by the hasty visit, Ruth left the widow to her nap and wandered out the northern gate. Had Pervis told no one about the *nux vomica*?

A stream of smoke darkened the sky above the New Field, billowing from a bright orange bonfire. Infected carcasses were dragged to the flames with gloved hands.

Farther to the south, in a corner of the Old Field, a second fire flared. Plows lay abandoned, the men shouting back and forth.

When school let out, the children were forbidden to leave the palisade. From the lookouts they watched the bonfires excitedly. Mr. Bassett, a severe look on his face, raced about the parade grounds, a letter clutched in his fist. He ran to the Paines' cabin, but found only the old lady sleeping.

Goody Blakeman, leaving from a visit to Baby Rebecca, hailed the schoolmaster, but he ignored her call, heading for the postern gate.

In the Old Field, Thomas Uffoot pointed him to the Sound. "She is gone to the bluffs," he said curtly. A gray sheep lay stiff at his feet.

Mr. Bassett stalked off, his swallow tails flapping behind him, his gaze set on Sewenhacky. At the first stand of cattails, he stopped short. Several gulls, their wide wings bent at awkward angles, lay together in a clump of marsh grass. Veering around them, he hurried on, but Ruth was up the coast at the shell heap, well beyond the range of his sight.

Late in the afternoon, Pervis returned from the woods. At sunrise, keeping downwind, he had planted portions of a freshly quartered lamb within range of suspected wolf dens. At noon, when the wind shifted, the wolves had come forth. While they were distracted, Pervis entered their dens, crawling down sandy tunnels beneath large boulders and stumps. The quick checks had confirmed his worst fears.

In the middle of the parade grounds he enountered Reverend Blakeman and Nicolas Knell, each party seeking the other. Pervis spoke first, giving the Reverend no chance.

"For each wolf that lies dead and buried, sir, there be *two* wolf cubs born." His voice was rusty and almost inaudible. He pulled his red knit cap about his ears.

The Reverend's bushy eyebrows arched to the top of his forehead, as somber and black as his spring frock coat. Bonfires leaped beyond the palisade.

"It be nature's way," Nicolas Knell said gravely.

"Nay, Mr. Knell, it be the Devil's!" The Reverend's voice thundered about the home-lots. "See how Satan wakes from his winter slumber! O, Stratford, look to thy soul!"

John Blakeman came running from the Watchhouse, several members of the train-band at his heels. Pervis dusted his buckskins and stepped quietly away.

That evening, the Paines' cabin door rattled with brisk knocking. The widow was asleep, Ruth tending the fire.

Pervis peeked from the loft. "If that be Moses Wheeler," he said, "I come directly."

But it was Charles Bassett, his hair disheveled and sticking to a sweaty brow. Wet sand clung to the legs of his gray suit. He held a letter rolled in his fist. He stared long and hard at Ruth.

"I must see Mr. Pervis," he said. Pausing to catch his breath, he looked beyond Ruth into the cabin. "Please tell him who calls!"

Hearing the voice, the wolf man dropped from the rafters to the nail keg. "Well, well," he mocked. "Mr. Schoolmaster!"

Charles Bassett remained on the stone front step. "I wish a word with you, sir, at my quarters!"

"And where might that be, sonny boy?"

"At the Meeting House, annexed to my classroom."

"What? Will ye take me to school?"

Charles Bassett looked to Ruth as if for help. She stood stiffly inside the doorway, her lips parted, red hair tangled about her shoulders.

She turned to the nail keg, her voice strained. "It . . . be never too late to learn, sir."

Pervis laughed—or winced—briefly. "What? Will the wench school me too!" He tugged his red knit cap about his ears. "So be it! But I will visit the ferry keeper by and by!" Grabbing his fringed jacket, he followed the schoolmaster into the dark spring night.

Ruth watched their shadows recede into the parade grounds, then wrapped herself in her rust-red pelt. Falling into bed, she tried to sleep.

In the morning, waking early, she found the loft empty. Pervis was gone. His strange sack, his traps, his shillings gone, too. The Reverend called again for Pervis as rumors spread, and by noontime the news was known to all: Pervis, the wolf man, vanished!

Reverend Blakeman huddled with Nicolas Knell on the banks of the Pootatuck. "Can a man disappear into the ethers? Have not witches changed men into wolves?"

"Patience, sir," Nicolas Knell advised. "Wait for signs!" He tugged his beard hard with both hands.

Bonfires blazed anew in the outlying fields, piled high with poisoned carcasses. The pastures remained empty, the cows and sheep confined to their pens.

Dismissing class early, Charles Bassett hurried across the parade grounds to the cabin in the corner of the palisade. He spent the afternoon and evening there, and the following day a new rumor spread through Stratford: the schoolmaster to marry Ruth Paine!

24.

Goody Bassett

THE children were unable to sit still. Whenever the school-master turned his back, there was poking and whispering. "The teacher will marry Ruth Paine!"

"It is only proper for a woman to marry," Deliverance Blake-man defended, "and bear children, like Goody Thomson." She spoke quickly over her shoulder from the first row of benches. "Our Mr. Bassett—"

"Nay, the widow shall box his ears!"

"They'll eat pine cones for breakfast!"

"And wolf meat at noon!"

"And howl by the light of the moon!"

Charles Bassett turned sharply from the small slate board he had attached to the front of the elevated pulpit, and the children quieted instantly. Although he had been poised to write for several minutes, he had not yet made a mark.

Turning again, he glimpsed Moses Wheeler in the doorway trying to get his attention. The large plank door had been left open, showing the Pootatuck beyond, its green banks washed in the bright air of spring. The burly man had left his ferry unattended.

"Recess for now," Charles Bassett announced suddenly. "One quarter hour. And see that ye are settled upon thy return!"

There was a rush for the door, the buckskinned ferry keeper

leaping aside as the children fled their benches. Within seconds they were scattered along the river.

Setting the chalk on the crude desk beside the pulpit, Charles Bassett noted the level of the sand in the brassbound hourglass, then marched from the Meeting House. He dusted his hands in front of Moses Wheeler. "A fine day, sir. A fine spring day!"

"Good God Gravy, Bassett, what goes on?"

"Have you no eyes, sir?"

"Aye, and ears that like not what they hear!"

The schoolmaster folded his arms across his chest. "Why, I hear only the children at play, Mr. Wheeler. Except for Deliverance, who reads her Bible in the shade of yon willow. How she favors her father!"

The huge man shook his head. "Then listen more closely, Bassett. Do ye not hear the lowin' of the cattle about the home-lots? The Reverend has ordered the livestock to the parade grounds for pasture. The sheep will ruin the grass within a week! The train-band has set the fields aflame; acres to be scorched and plowed under!"

"To purge the infectious malady."

"*Plague*, sir; it be the Devil's plague!"

"Is that what you hear?"

"The Reverend speaks of witchcraft."

The schoolmaster clasped his hands behind his back and fiddled with the swallow tails of his suit coat. "The eyes and ears may bear infection, too, Mr. Wheeler. Is that not so?"

"The tongue to boot, for all thy talk!"

Charles Bassett stepped toward the river. Three gulls glided high in the sunlight, following the blue of the Pootatuck toward the darker waters of the Sound. A lone tern perched on the wharf.

"Stratford has been a prisoner of winter; nothing but spinning and weaving and darning socks and repairing hoes and plows. But now, the sap is running." The schoolmaster paused thoughtfully, staring at his feet. "I would talk, sir, but for thy cider jug, which repeateth like a pirate's parrot what it hears."

The burley man in buckskin shook his head. "Come, Bassett, my jug is dry!"

"And yet Pervis would keep a rendezvous."

"He's vanished, sir! My tongue is stilled. I fear the stocks —and banishment."

"Fear instead the rampant imagination."

The ferry keeper raised a thick fist. "Good God Gravy, Bassett, quit thy philosophy and speak like a man! Ruth lies abed, sobbing her soul away. The widow defends her with her—"

"Crying still?"

"Aye, I've come directly."

Charles Bassett shifted his gaze to the rippling river. "My duties keep me here 'til afternoon."

"And is it true, sir, that you—"

"—will marry the girl?"

Moses Wheeler nodded.

"Aye, I will take her for my bride, to lead about and instruct her, to keep her as the apple of my eye."

"And be she willin', sir?"

"Aye, she is willing."

"Then why does she sob so abed?" Moses Wheeler stood on the riverbank like an oak tree, like a threatening giant. "Ye will do her no harm, sir. I have been as her father!"

"And that is the very word that grates."

"*Father?*"

"Exactly so."

Thin gray smoke canceled the sweet smell of pine. West of the palisade, members of the train-band stood about with rakes and shovels, guarding the low flames that swept across the New Field. Others stood ready with their plows.

"Those Dutchmen, Mr. Wheeler, that ye so lately ferried through, brought letters from Massachusetts Bay."

"One for the Reverend reported witchcraft in England."

"And one, sir, was from my mentor in Harvard."

"Thy what?"

"An aged friend in Massachusetts Bay. I had written him of our progress in Stratford not long after Mr. Pervis arrived. But what seemed at first an innocent exchange of news hath taken a turn of the utmost import. Would that the snows had not delayed his words!" The schoolmaster settled himself. His voice had soared. "And yet I trust his words have not advanced my suit unfairly."

Deliverance Blakeman looked up from the nearby willow. The schoolmaster was intent in conversation. There was time yet to read. She was reciting verses to herself from the Book of Ruth: " 'All the city of my people doth know that thou art a virtuous woman.' "

Beside her in the grass lay another book, the *Actes & Monuments Of These Latter Perilous Days*, published by John Foxe in 1563. The drab volume detailed the hideous disfigurements of the religious martyrs and served as a model for all Puritan children. She could recount its tales from memory and knew the moral well: life was to be piously endured, until the approach of joyous death.

The broad brow of Moses Wheeler wrinkled fiercely. "Good God Gravy, Bassett, out with it!"

"But thy tongue, sir."

"My jug is dry and my tongue is still! Need I tack it to the wall in proclamation?"

Gray smoke curled in the breeze. Yellow flames were visible through narrow gaps in the palisade. At the river, the tern left the wharf.

"A woman died last fall in Plymouth, following a fever. But before she died, in order to prepare herself for Heaven and cleanse her soul of a heavy guilt, she confessed a sin that had been a long-guarded secret. A child born to her out of wedlock had been put into the care of a childless couple. That child, Mr. Wheeler, was Ruth Paine."

Disappointment fell across the ferry keeper's face. "You dawdle, Mr. Bassett, on what has long been suspected. It is the widow's silliness to fancy Ruth her own child. The mind of an old and lonesome woman—"

"The child was given with the understanding that it would be taken from Massachusetts Bay, from the eyes of its mother and the site of her sin. And so it was raised in Windsor. That much, as ye say, has been surmised." The schoolmaster watched the tern disappear upriver. "But twenty-two years ago, Mr. Wheeler, Plymouth was beset by wolves, and Massachusetts Bay enacted a bounty law, the first such provision of its kind in the Americas. As she lay near death, the woman of Plymouth named a bounty hunter as her partner in sin, and now her family seeks the man in retribution."

Charles Bassett looked up into the large wide eyes of Moses Wheeler. Children were running from the river toward the Meeting House.

"Pervis?"

"The father of Ruth."

"Good God Gravy!"

"A fate worse than any legend of the Greeks." The schoolmaster tugged at his stiff collar, at a loss to explain. "When I showed her the letter, she sat abed and stared at the loft, as if that hole in the roof were a chimney through which her life had gone up in smoke. And then she sobbed. Oh, Wheeler, how she sobbed! I offered comfort, her will and spirit broken. 'Take care of me, sir,' was all she said."

"And so ye invited poor Ruth to marry you."

"In so many words, sir. I know it were in haste, and yet I trust that I have not advanced my suit unfairly. I have long loved the girl, in my fashion."

The children were almost upon them, shoving each other along.

"I fear yer fashion, sir, suits Stratford like yer Greeks!"

●　　●　　●

Ruth sobbed until she fell asleep, then woke and sobbed again. Why had he fled? Where was the love? He had fled before her birth, but why flee again, now that he knew her?

Knew her. Had almost known her, as Adam had known Eve. And how she had desired the knowing, all the knowledge in those deep-set eyes! If thoughts were worse than deeds, she had sinned a thousand fold.

And yet—oh, why had he fled!

Ruth rolled to the log wall, wrapped in her wolf pelt. Anna Paine stood above her, broom in hand. The widow knew only that her daughter was upset. She did not know the cause or that Pervis had left. Indeed, her eyes went from the door to the opening in the loft, half expecting the strange man to appear in his red knit cap. Though muffled and choked, Ruth's sobbing struck her ears as clearly as the Meeting House bell, driving the puzzled glaze from her eyes. She understood that it was her turn to protect and care for her daughter as best she could.

And how did Pervis feel? Ruth wondered. Safe? Appalled? Indifferent? What did he think of his daughter? Did he approve? Was she not his very spit and image? How absurd for the two of them not to have noticed: the same angular limbs, the sharp nose, the red hair, the fine bones! Was there no time for greeting before leave-taking? Or did he feel, as she herself sensed, that hello would make good-bye impossible?

And yet—oh, where was the love?

"The choice," Mr. Bassett had said, seeking her out on the very day that the wolf man had fled, "was *his*, Ruth, his alone." Confronted with the truth, he had chosen to flee. The alternatives were too confusing, revolving like a spinning-wheel, as twisted as the threads from a warped loom.

Rolling from the wall, Ruth opened her eyes. Her face was red and streaked with tears. The noise of her own sobbing startled her. Anna Paine stood above her like a fortress.

What was the hour? Mr. Bassett—Charles—would be coming soon, straight from his classroom. To make plans for the . . .

marriage. She would be married, like Anne Wines, taken for a
bride.

Taken up. Taken away. Taken care of, all for the simple nodding of her head. And once wed, there would be no fear of Pervis, of her father, of ever knowing him.

Oh, Charles, so full of life! How easy to make him happy!
How he dreaded growing old alone! And so it must have been
with Sergeant Nichols. Dear Francis, forgive me. Forgive . . .

And yet—what of the love?

25.

The Pestle

CONCEALED by tall cattails and marsh grass, the young Pequannock watched the confused settlers plowing the blackened earth of the Old Field. He watched for hours. The White Man of the black coat, the one with blacksnakes above his eyes, paced the smoldering ground, shouting at the others. "Though we bury Satan's scourge, yet he sleepeth not! O Stratford, look to thy soul!"

The words flew like strange and noisy birds, and the report was carried back of White Men scurrying like ants, of gates left open, of firesticks set aside like water buckets.

The sachems nodded, listening carefully: Queriheag, Towtanomow, Ansantaway. The boy had done well. He would soon wear a pigtail above the ear.

William Beardsley, current magistrate to the General Court at Hartford, married Charles Bassett and Ruth Paine several days after Pervis disappeared. There were no announcements. Mr. Bassett would not wait. And Ruth, who attended the Sabbath irregularly, using the widow's health as an excuse, was content not to have her name singled out for public discussion.

On the day of her marriage, her nose was still red from crying and she saw the world through glassy eyes, not the radiant glaze of a spring-time bride.

Although the day was warm, she took her wolf pelt for a

shawl. Bassett wore his swallowtail suit. Anna Paine slept soundly in the corner, the magistrate speaking above her snore.

When the magistrate left, the schoolmaster suggested that Ruth—Goody Bassett—take a quick stroll about the parade grounds to revive her senses.

"And why not stop by Goody Thomson's to see Baby Rebecca? After all, what is marriage for?"

He himself would stay behind and prepare a wedding drink of sassafras tea and ground nutmeg, laced with a spit of cider from Moses Wheeler's jug.

Ruth agreed, eager to get outdoors. Eager to flee.

As she hurried from the widow's cabin, she thought of her father. What trick of the Reverend's great God had brought him to Stratford to dwell beside her? And yet, she knew, it was not at all surprising. The entire Connecticut Colony numbered only in the hundreds, and those who were not the strictest of Puritans had a way of seeking out their own.

But what of the love? *The love?*

The tall oaks that ringed the parade grounds gave dappled shade to the bright afternoon, but Ruth kept in the sunlight, making her way about the cattle and sheep. Their eyes were as cloudy as her own. A deep chill sank into her bones. She feared the sunset, feared her wedding night.

She stopped before the large slate stones that made a path to the Thomsons' cabin. Jon Thomson and his sons were off plowing the last section of the Old Field. Baby Rebecca screamed through an open window.

Hesitating on the doorstep, Ruth knocked lightly. What if Goody Blakeman were there? What if—But the door opened and Goody Thomson stood alone, in a long black dress, her dark hair pulled back into a heavy knot.

Ruth pushed a stray lock behind her ear. She had left without her white cap, and suddenly her own hair seemed offensive. "I am married now," she said quietly. "I would see thy Rebecca."

The stony face of Goody Thomson softened. A wide smile parted her thin lips. "Why, child, do come in! Why, Goody Bassett! So newly wed and yet so—"

Baby Rebecca screamed.

"Come in, Goody Bassett, and see the baby! See how children bear the light of Christ himself!"

The cabin was plainly furnished: a pine table, four rough chairs, a large bed in the corner, twin pallets for the boys in the loft. Baby Rebecca's cradle, fashioned from the lengthwise half of a nail keg, sat by the fireplace, directly opposite the door.

Ruth crossed the room quickly. How solid the pine planks felt beneath her feet in contrast to the widow's soft earth floor!

The swaddled infant lay screeching. Tears streaked its fat cheeks.

Goody Thomson beamed, awaiting words of praise, but Ruth was silent. Was this how she herself had looked when carried to Windsor from Massachusetts Bay? What could her mother have been like, to abandon a helpless child? Where was the—?

Suddenly there was a rush at the door and a Red Man raced in, his shrill whoop shattering Ruth's thoughts. He was naked except for buckskin leggings. His bright eyes flashed, his arms aloft as if in warning. A second Red Man entered just as swiftly, catching the first with a tomahawk to the back of the skull, sending him crashing to the floor where he died almost at once.

Then the other was gone, out the door and over the palisade wall.

Goody Thomson fainted straight away, dropping like a pile of rags. Baby Rebecca screamed. The Red Man's black hair was thick with blood. Ruth grabbed him by the shoulders and rolled him over. A leather pouch that hung from his neck slid across his chest.

Ruth shuddered, kneeling at his side. Sharp lines creased the leather of his face. The eyes were open, sharp and dark, the very eyes that had watched her from the woods.

Nimrod. It was Nimrod!

Jon Thomson appeared in the doorway, out of breath. He ran to his wife. Baby Rebecca screamed again, and Ruth fled into the gathering crowd.

As darkness fell, the wolves began to howl, breaking their long silence for the first time since winter. The howling began as a low, throaty growl that rose quickly to a fierce, high whine, breaking off abruptly at its peak. The volume hinted of a hundred wolves.

Nicolas Knell came alone to the Reverend's study. "And what of this Red Man, dead at our doorstep!"

"The Devil strikes within the home-lots no sooner than his scourge is plowed under!"

"A sign, sir, most certainly a sign!"

"How the crying of the wolves sounds like laughter!"

"And Pervis gone!"

"We dare not put the livestock to pasture!"

"A heathen falls dead before an innocent child!"

"But Goodwife Thomson is most pious and devout!"

"Dead at the feet of Ruth Paine!"

"Our Goodwife Bassett!"

"They say he moved as if to signal!"

"Aye, but what the message?"

"A heathen kills his brother—"

"—and each a devil!"

The narrow study seemed cramped, confined.

"Let us go now to Ruth!"

"Nay, Knell, it is her nuptial night."

Suddenly Jane Blakeman pushed the study door open. "Adam!" she cried. "Go now!"

The Reverend's eyes flashed with anger. "Jane!"

"No time for squabble," Nicolas Knell insisted. "Let us go!"

The Reverend hesitated a moment, then shoved his books

aside and pressed from the study, Nicolas Knell hard at his heels. They went down the narrow stairway and out the front door, but their progress was halted, abruptly, on the porch. A bright red streak rose in the sky from the river, then suddenly disappeared.

"Comet!" the Reverend cried. "The very heavens lend a—"

"Fire arrow!" Nicolas Knell shouted.

The flaming shaft had buried itself into the roof of the Meeting House. Moments later a small fire flared in the thatch below the bell tower.

"The water buckets, Knell, quickly!"

It was a drill that had been practiced often: to the rain barrel and thence to the roof. The Reverend followed Nicolas Knell into the Meeting House and up the back stairs, and within minutes the threatening blaze was extinguished.

"God be praised!" the Reverend cried.

"To the river!" Nicolas Knell replied. "Canoe!" Grabbing the rope in the bell tower, he sounded the general alarm.

In the deeper darkness of the riverbank, a lone canoe fought the current upstream. Passing the northern gate, it broke for the safety of the opposite shore, plainly visible in the reflected moonlight. But John Blakeman and his train-band arrived on the run and dropped the marauders in their seats with a blast of musket fire.

The errant canoe was retrieved like a wounded duck.

"Warriors of Ansantaway," John Blakeman announced, "from upriver. Ansantaway, the instigator!"

The faces of the two Red Men who lay doubled over in the darkness were streaked with a mixture of berry juice and clay.

"Painted devils!" the Reverend exclaimed, coming at a trot across the graveyard. "Bring torches! There be no sleep to-night!"

Jon Thomson sat awake before a blazing fire, his two sons at his side, his musket trained on the door. In the corner bed his wife squeezed their infant to her breast, growing more restless with each cry of the wolves.

The wolves had come again, as suddenly as Pervis had disappeared. A heathen Red Man had fallen dead within his door. Jon Thomson had been afraid to answer the call of the general alarm.

Elsewhere in Stratford the women and children quivered in their beds. No one slept.

And at first light, as Reverend Blakeman and Nicolas Knell crossed the parade grounds to Anna Paine's cabin, John Blakeman came running from Watchhouse Hill. He carried what looked to be a large log against his chest.

"Look, father! These are found without the gate!"

He held forth a bundle of arrows, feathered hickory shafts with triangular flint heads, bound in a long brown snakeskin.

Members of the train-band stood along the palisade, their muskets at the ready.

"The skin of a copperhead," Nicolas Knell said.

The Reverend winced. "A poisonous viper!"

His son was trembling. "Each arrow is different. They are the arrows of many tribes."

Nicolas Knell extended a tentative hand to the bundle. "An ancient custom. A symbol of defiance. Ansantaway, no doubt, pricks them on."

Reverend Blakeman grabbed the arrows from his son. "Then let us answer with ball and shot! Have thy men, John, fire a volley into the heathen forest!"

The crack of muskets split the morning air, puffs of smoke drifting across the home-lots. Startled livestock bumped each other within the pens, the field spaniels yelping. The settlers rushed from their cabins in bedclothes.

"The dead Red Man," the Reverend said as he headed for the small home-lot in the corner of the palisade, "came in warning."

Nicolas Knell strained to keep up. They crossed the line of oaks on the edge of the parade grounds. "To warn Ruth."

"A Devil's compact!"

The lone window of the cabin was shuttered tight. A reddish-brown cow grazed quietly in the side yard, somehow free of its pen.

Reverend Blakeman knocked hard on the door. When no one answered, he knocked again. Then he tried the latch, and the door swung open.

Anna Paine lay sleeping in the far corner. Ruth stood in the center of the room. She was staring dumbly at a stone pestle on the nail keg, where Charles Bassett, while his goodwife was visiting Goody Thomson, had ground nutmeg for a nuptial drink.

Testing it, he had died immediately on Ruth's narrow bed and spent his wedding night in a puddle of his own vomit, his face contorted in a hideous grin.

26.

The Stratford Devil

SUMMONED from the ferry, Moses Wheeler draped the schoolmaster over his shoulder and carried him out. A mob of settlers pressed against the cabin, restrained by members of the trainband.

"A spell were upon him," Goody Blakeman whispered. "He ran about the home-lots confusedly and heeded not my cry!"

Goody Thomson held her infant above the crowd. "She brings the heathen to prey on innocent souls!"

Baby Rebecca screamed.

Francis Nichols arrived on the run. "Anne lies ill!" he called. "Told of Ruth, she swooned in a fever!"

John Blakeman backed against the door, his musket braced across his chest. He tried hard to avoid his mother's eyes.

Inside, Ruth stared at the nail keg. Anna Paine breathed heavily beneath her stack of blankets. The Reverend stepped forward, Nicolas Knell at his heels.

"Touch me not!" Ruth said. Her eyes were red, her hair pulled and tangled about her face.

"Lay thyself open, child, and make way for thy minister to do thee good."

"Have ye permission to *visit*, sir?"

The Reverend hesitated. "Think of thy namesake, Ruth the Moabite, as she cut and bound the sheaves. Imitate her spirit and—"

"*Per*haps I have a *vision* of my own."

"What? Has thou denied thy Saviour?"

178

"Such treachery is evident, sir."

The Reverend glanced over his shoulder at Nicolas Knell. "Ruth, do ye know thy holy Father?"

"Aye, but my father knows me not."

"Do ye know the Truth?"

"I have seen it."

"Where and how?"

"Writ in sand."

"Writ in sand?"

"Aye, writ by a bird."

"Did it speak?"

"It spoke with its tail."

"And do ye hear it now, Ruth?"

"Nay, it has flown."

"The Lord Jesus Christ hath broke the Old Serpent's head!"

"What do ye say?"

"I say the Lord Jesus Christ hath broke the Old Serpent's head!"

"I hear not a word."

"Well then, mind me and ye shall know what ye can hear. A snake, Ruth. Can ye hear?"

"Aye."

"Well, an Old Snake. Can ye hear?"

"What of an old snake?"

"It lies broke. Can ye hear?"

"Aye, and what then?"

"Why, who broke it?"

Ruth looked suddenly from the pestle to the loft, speaking as if through the roof. "Wretch! Ye make my heart cold! Are you God? Do ye say that thou art Christ? Pray, go about thy business if thou art Christ! And yet I tell thee plainly, ye shall be none of *my* Christ. Nay, thou art a beast!"

"Ruth!"

"Fine promises! Bestow a husband on me? A husband? What? A Devil! I shall then be finely fitted for a husband!"

"Ruth!"

"Fine clothes! What? Rags to cover me! And what if I am fatherless? Nay, I have not been fatherless!"

"Ruth! Do ye speak to the Devil?"

"Nay!"

"Mock our Lord?"

"Nay!"

"Pervert the Psalms?"

"*Pervert?*"

"Aye!"

"Don't meddle with me!"

"Do ye serve a Hard Master?"

"What?"

"Shall we pray?"

"To my father?"

"Aye!"

"Pervert my father?"

"What?"

"I piss on him!"

The Reverend recoiled, and Ruth broke into sobs. Anna Paine woke suddenly and kicked her blankets away, her dark eyes wide and clear. She reached for her broom, and Reverend Blakeman and Nicolas Knell broke for the door.

Condemned for witchcraft, Goody Bassett was confined to the widow's cabin. John Blakeman guarded the door. John Haynes, Governor of the Connecticut Colony, arrived for the trial on the first day of May, accompanied by two of his magistrates.

The settlers squeezed into every bench of the Meeting House and lined the walls in triple rows. Despite the warm spring day, the plank door was kept shut. Train-band sentinels listened from the roof.

Only Francis Nichols was absent. He was tending to his wife, who lay afflicted with fever, her frail soul, like that of Mary Nichols before her, struggling for life.

The Governor was a short, rotund man with broad side-whiskers, his gray hair tied at the nape of his neck with a black velvet ribbon. In other circumstances he might have cut a jovial figure, but in court he was somber and grave.

"Since Almighty God hath given most certain and plain indication in matters of this kind, it is not only the saving duty of all private men to take diligent and wary notice thereof, but it is the charge of princes and magistrates to fulfill the commanded execution of God's holy wrath and vengeance."

He spoke from the elevated pulpit, Goody Bassett at the crude desk beside him. She was staring at the brassbound hourglass, her nose red and chapped, eyes glazed, hair undone.

Nicolas Knell, seated with the Governor's magistrates, nodded vigorously. Anna Paine occupied the first bench, constrained by Reverend Blakeman and his son. Several rows behind, on the women's side of the aisle, Jane Blakeman watched intently with Goody Thomson. Baby Rebecca was at her mother's breast.

Moses Wheeler kept well to the rear, standing just in front of the doorway. Events had transpired too quickly for his comprehension. He had carried the frigid corpse of Charles Bassett from the widow's cabin, then dug a hole for the casket in the riverside graveyard. Had the schoolmaster confided only to him? Pervis was gone, obviously fled. Knowledge of that, and of the reason for Ruth's deep grief, could well implicate the man who would speak of it. Such familiarity, as the Reverend's long lectures had made clear, would mean certain condemnation, a fate as dark as the gnawing guilt of keeping silent.

The large man turned, as if for advice, to Jon Thomson, who was wedged against the doorframe beside him.

"If she confesses," the shorter man whispered, "there be no need for trial. If not, they'll torture. Confession maketh execution legal."

"The pain of torture is nothing to what the Devil will make her suffer!"

"Hush!" Jon Thomson gazed above the heads in front of him, straining to see.

"If the times be such," the Governor continued, "that the authors of such acts escape and are encouraged in their wickedness and are made use of to take away the lives of others; this is worse than making vain the law of God."

Again, Nicolas Knell nodded. Reverend Blakeman was perspiring profusely, his eyes darting from the Governor to Ruth. But Ruth sat quietly, deaf to all sound.

"Read the charges!" the Governor ordered.

One of the Governor's magistrates, as long and thin as the Governor was round, and dressed in a similar black gown, moved abruptly to the side of the pulpit. The length of paper he unrolled, embossed with the dark seal of the colony, shook in his hands. His voice was almost shrill.

" 'Whereas the bounty hunter known as Pervis, God's own ardent defender against the wolves of Satan, hath so summarily disappeared from Stratford's gate; and whereas the aforesaid bounty hunter hath lodged these several months in the midst of the accused; and whereas Mr. Charles Bassett, God's own devoted schoolmaster on civilization's frontier, hath suffered so agonizing and untimely a death, within a few brief hours of marriage to the accused, and in the very dwelling from which the aforesaid bounty hunter hath mysteriously flown; and whereas the heathen Pequannock known as Nimrod, struck by a fellow painted Devil, hath fallen dead at the feet of the accused, whither he had come in warning of planned pagan hostilities; thus the charges against the accused, one Ruth Paine of Stratford, so recently known as the Goodwife Bassett, are threefold:

" 'Firstly, *lycanthropy*: wherein the accused possesseth the magical ability to assume the form and charm of a wolf, transforming others, namely the aforesaid bounty hunter, to that guise for her own pleasure; witnesseth the wolf pelt she hath worn since childhood;

" 'Secondly, *murder most foul*: wherein the accused hath sucked the breath from a living soul, namely the aforesaid Charles Bassett, for her own pleasure; witnesseth the cruel corpse that now rests in its grave;

" 'And thirdly, *willful communion with the Prince of Darkness*: wherein the accused has trafficked in knowledge with the instruments of Satan; witnesseth the corpse of Nimrod, purged to ashes by bonfire, within the bounds of Stratford's palisade.

" 'And know ye further that though these charges be threefold, they be at the root but one charge: the exercise of those dark powers known as witchcraft. Ruth Paine, Goodwife Bassett, a witch!

" 'Thus these charges, as writ by the Reverend Adam Blakeman and the leading elders of the town of Stratford in the Colony of Connecticut, are subscribed thereto before the Governor John Haynes, on this first day of May in the year of our Lord, sixteen hundred and fifty-one.' "

The magistrate drew a deep breath, and as the charges were reiterated—lycanthropy, murder most foul, willful communion with the Prince of Darkness—Ruth sat quietly, watching the white sand fall through the hourglass so quick and free. Was that a black grain there—just then—amidst the white? How quickly buried! No chance among the white sands of Ipswich. The overwhelming whiteness of purity and innocence will always smother such a black grain. And yet, when the glass be turned, would not the black grain pass through time again? Would not future generations see such grains?

The magistrate sat down. The Governor looked from Ruth to the crowd before him. "Since the accused hath elected silence, is there no one who will speak in her defense?"

Heads turned in a general rumbling. Moses Wheeler squirmed, all eyes upon him, then the room fell quiet. Anna Paine, to the surprise of everyone, stood suddenly, twisting from the grip of the Reverend and his son.

She wore a clean apron, and her iron-gray hair was tucked

forcefully beneath her cap. Moving forward slowly, she bent low over the desk at which Ruth sat.

Ruth spoke to her softly, lips hardly moving, for the first time in days. "Mother, would ye have me for a witch?"

The widow glared for a moment at the Governor. "Nay, child. Thou art but a trading-post baby, swapped at Windsor for butter and salt." Then she turned to the sea of faces, her eyes fixed on Moses Wheeler in the rear.

But instead of the burly ferry keeper, she saw Jonas Paine. Old husband. Saw him clearly, out of the past, and her voice began to rise steadily, loud, sour, and deliberate, from some ancient reserve of strength.

"People of Stratford! Ye speak of the Red Man! Ye speak of wolves! But were ye ever invited to Sandy Hollow? Nay! Ye came on the blood of Jonas Paine! Will ye now feast on the blood of his daughter?"

The widow's thick hands flew stiffly to her hips, her feet planted wide. "Ye say the Black Man himself has come to Stratford? I say nay, but we have a Blake-Man!" A stubby finger shook at the Reverend. "Yonder sits the Stratford Devil!"

Baby Rebecca screamed. The settlers jumped up. Anna Paine lowered her head and rushed the front bench, but John Blakeman blocked her way.

Moses Wheeler raced up the aisle and locked his arm about the widow's throat. She was dragged, struggling, from the Meeting House.

"Raised from an infant! Late to childbearing!"

A breath of warm spring air blew in from the Pootatuck, then the heavy plank door slammed shut.

The Reverend dusted his frock coat and sat down again, his eyebrows quivering. "See how she sends her spirit out! Even now our young Anne Nichols lies afflicted!"

Ruth put her head to the desk and sobbed.

"Be seated!" the Governor ordered. "The woman is old and sick. The accused will stand before the bench."

The room quieted to a hum. Ruth didn't move. At a nod from the Governor, two regulars dispatched themselves from the rear of the aisle, came forward, and raised Ruth from her seat, one on each arm. Then the Governor's voice, in a sudden change of tone, turned fatherly.

"Child, ye have heard the charges presented against thee, and yet ye have elected silence. This is the final time to be granted by this court for your response. Do ye deny the charges, child?"

Ruth stood before the pulpit, her back to the crowd, staring at the thick plank floor. What a foundation had been constructed over the earth! She could remember many Sabbath days when the floor had been frozen mud, when her legs dangled from the rear bench too short to let her touch down. What a building had been constructed at Cupheag! A place of worship, a schoolhouse, and now a court.

Such thoughts cleared her head, the mist rising from her eyes like morning vapor. Then she thought of Anna Paine, dragged away in her defense, and her lips tightened.

"Child, do ye deny such charges?"

The Governor's voice was losing its soft corners.

Ruth's reply was scarcely audible. "Where truth is not present, sir, there be no need for denial."

"Louder!" the Reverend Blakeman bellowed, hardly seated on the first wooden bench. "Let the citizens of Stratford hear all testimony!"

The Governor was adamant. "Silence, sir! Thy authority stops with this court! Have ye not called us to Stratford?" He looked to Ruth again. "Child, do ye hear me. Will ye confess?"

Despite the advantage of the elevated pulpit, Ruth felt the eyes of the Governor level with hers.

"Where truth is not present, sir, there be no need for con—"

"Proceed to the examination of secret marks!"

"Amen!" the Reverend shouted, and "Amen!" rang through the hall.

"Signs of intimacies! Strange teats where she doth suckle her familiars, the incubi and sundry imps!" The Governor waved at the captain of the train-band. "Strip the girl!"

The settlers moved to the edge of their benches. Ruth raised her chin defiantly, pushing a damp lock of hair from her face. John Blakeman came forward from his father's side, his hand on the hilt of his sword.

Ruth stood firm. "Nay, sir. He will touch me not."

Governor Haynes blinked. "What? Do ye refuse examination?"

"Of all men, sir—he hath lusted. I have felt his eyes burning in my soul."

John Blakeman laughed. "She hath denied me the hour of the day!"

"And the day of the week, Master Blakeman, for thy lust hath burned through the years." Ruth turned to the Reverend. "One may sin in thought as well as deed. Is that not, sir, what ye have preached these many years? Be that not writ in the Book that instructs us? Pray, sir. Inquire of his thoughts. Glare not at me but at thy son!"

The settlers rumbled. Jane Blakeman stood up abruptly across the aisle, tugged back to her seat by the arm of Goody Thomson. The Reverend and his son stood open-mouthed.

"Enough!" the Governor cried. "Do ye refuse examination, Goody Bassett? I consider denial an admission of guilt!"

Ruth spun about and put both hands on the pulpit, her hair flying from her shoulders like ribbons. "I will not stand naked before the men of Stratford! I am a goodwife!" Her voice suddenly left her. She had never stood naked before any man, not even her husband. Poor Charles!

The swirling pine grain in the pulpit blurred before her eyes as her mind fled to the Pootatuck, to the clearing in the pines upstream. There, years ago, nakedness had seemed a blessing. And yet no man had ever seen her naked. No man had ever touched her . . . except Nimrod.

Nimrod! The very thought alarmed her. Was *that* why he had watched from the woods for her all these years? Was Nimrod a victim of the same dark blood that stirred the eyes of John Blakeman? If so, she were better off dead.

The Governor looked in desperation to his magistrates. Then Nicolas Knell stood and pointed behind the pulpit to the door that led to the annex, the living quarters of the former school-master.

Moses Wheeler, catching the gesture, raised a fist. "Aye, Governor! Who among us would gaze at the Devil's body? I, for one, will not face such temptation, lest the house of God become a bloody brothel!"

Murmurs of assent rippled forward through the rows. The Governor, staring at the Reverend, debated with himself. And Ruth, as if the matter had been decided when the ferry keeper spoke, walked quietly to the annex door.

The Reverend's wife was ordered to examine her.

27.

The Lesson

GOVERNOR John Haynes sentenced Goody Bassett to be hanged from the tallest tree in Stratford. The evidence was overwhelming, further trial unnecessary.

"Let her hanging," he declared, "be at once the torture and execution of sentence. If she confess in the meanwhile, then God be praised!"

"And let the hanging," Reverend Blakeman argued, "be outside the palisade in the forest, the very land of heathen spirits, as a lesson to the Red Man and the wolves!"

Leading a scouting party west of the New Field, John Blakeman returned exuberant. "A clearing stands beyond a twisting brook, a ledge of granite intervening, a magnificent oak overhead. It lends a sturdy branch for the hangman's noose!" He stepped to his father's side. "Hath the goodwife recanted?"

"Denies all allegations and confesses to nothing. But I will speak to her again, as duty dictates."

Ruth lay locked in the widow's cabin, sobbing on her bed. Anna Paine slept quietly, exhausted. Something had broken, had died within the widow, when she was dragged from the Meeting House. Her mind had retreated into the comfort of a thickening fog.

The Stratfordites ran about excitedly as Jane Blakeman recounted her tale of how Ruth had stood naked before her in the neat, narrow quarters of the schoolmaster, staring quietly at the books on his shelves. About her neck had hung a necklace of wolves' teeth! What sounder proof of lycanthropy? And high on her thigh, the very mark of the Devil, a passionate bite sustained in sexual intercourse!

The Reverend's wife spoke soberly yet indignantly, as if to erase from memory the slightest notion that her eldest son might have lusted after Ruth. If so, 'twere the Devil's doing!

"And her teats," she concluded, "the teats of a man!"

Goody Thomson pressed Baby Rebecca to her swollen bosom, to illustrate what proper breasts should be.

"I saw her kiss the proclamation of Captain Mason!" Thomas Hawley cried. "Kiss the very name of Nimrod! The Governor hath sent for the Captain to quell this latest uprising!"

Francis Nichols came forward briefly. His wife's fever had broken. "There is yet danger to her weakened constitution," he asserted, "but when the Stratford Devil hangs, full health will be restored!"

The settlers' sympathies flew out to him. How close he had come, those long years ago, to a fate as horrible as that of Charles Bassett!

The stories grew into wild rumors, each with a secret delight in the telling. Livestock wandered unattended about the home-lots, the sweet scent of spring mixed with the odor of dung. Ruth was brought from the cabin to the stocks.

"Recant or not," the Reverend said, "she hangs in the morning."

The Governor departed for Hartford, and the grassy clearing by the Meeting House drew a noisy crowd as Ruth was locked, head and wrists, into the broad planks. The children laughed, hurling pine cones from a distance, and Ruth shut her eyes against the sting. As she ignored their taunts, her defiance aroused more anger.

The settlers kept back, staring fearfully, the witch at bay. Moses Wheeler was the first to approach. He knelt by the stocks, his voice a tremulous whisper.

"Good God Gravy, child!"

"Mr. Wheeler, they will have my life."

"And I am threatened with banishment."

"Save thyself."

"Nay, I must help thee."

"There be no help, sir."

"Child!"

"Please go. Stand away. Save thyself."

"Ruth!"

"Get away. Please." Her eyes grew wide as she looked at the crowd and screamed. *"Begone, vile bugger, lest ye join me in hell!"*

The big man drew back in amazement and spat on the ground. The bold gesture drew wild cheers. Then others joined in, less afraid now, passing quickly, spitting at Ruth.

"So ye went to the woods," John Blakeman laughed, "to become a woman!"

Nicolas Knell cackled. "And the Devil proved a better lover than Charles Bassett!"

Goodman Peake brought the field spaniels forward, and one raised a leg to Ruth's backside.

The settlers roared with laughter.

And at sunset, when Ruth was returned to her cabin, Reverend Adam Blakeman visited for the last time. Anna Paine tossed fitfully in the corner. Her broom had been removed from the cabin, although she no longer sought it.

Ruth lay clutching her wolf pelt, her face to the log wall beside her bed. She had not sobbed since dragged from the stocks. Her eyes were clear.

The Reverend stood above her, speaking quietly.

"Prepare thy soul, Ruth. Go not with the Devil on the morrow."

"I care not where I go," Ruth answered. "Nor with whom. I wish only to die."

"For the sake of Stratford, Ruth, confess thyself."

"And yet I have done nothing."

"Recant. Deny the Devil. For Stratford's sake."

Ruth turned from the wall abruptly. "For Stratford's sake? Nay, sir; for *thine.*"

The Reverend stiffened. His eyebrows leaped, then settled

low on his forehead, his voice as hollow as a bucket. "Go not with the Devil on the morrow."

Anna Paine coughed in her bed and rolled over, and the Reverend turned to look at her broad, wrinkled face. How she had aged through the years in Stratford, keeping house for the Devil!

"If the wolf howls again," he said finally, "if the wolf howls, Ruth, when thou art gone, the eyes of Stratford will turn to thy mother." He nodded at the bed in the far corner.

Ruth closed her eyes. "Ye mistake me, sir. I am an orphan. No mother. No father."

"At the first indication of hostilities, when the next fire arrow crosses the palisade, all eyes will turn to the Widow Paine. It will be said that your spirit lingers still."

Ruth pushed her hair from her face and opened her eyes. "And will ye believe that, sir?"

The Reverend hesitated. "I have studied muchly, Ruth, for many years. There is precedent. I fear the Devil even now in thy words."

Ruth lay back and stared up through the heavy beams into the opening to the loft. Where was Pervis? Where had Pervis gone? Was there a place in America's woods for one such as he?

One thing was certain. There was no place for her.

Father gone, and mother, too. Parents but in name only. No obligation. *But what of the love?*

The widow coughed again, and Ruth looked to the corner. Dear Anna. Dear, dear Anna. Trading post wife and widow. Barren mother.

The Reverend's black brows were knit in confusion, but his eyes remained determined and clear.

"Provide for my mother, sir," Ruth said at last, "and lend thy strong arm always. The Devil dies with me. Tell Stratford I confess."

The Reverend clasped his hands high in the air. "God be praised!"

28.

The Granite Ledge

WILDFLOWERS bloomed in the New Field. Water filled the sunken brook beyond. Newly sprung underbrush made walking difficult. Leafy trees all but blocked the sun. Only in the clearing by the granite ledge was the May sky visible, a brilliant dome, a sign of Heaven itself.

Ruth felt calm. The Red Man and the wolves, she knew, had come this way. Here a squirrel had saved her from a rabid death. Here she had wandered unharmed. But as she was led to the oak from which the heavy rope hung, something within made her grip the granite ledge. She made no sound, no word or cries, but clutched the ledge tightly with both hands.

The people of Stratford, in a quiet ring about the clearing, watched anxiously until members of the train-band wrenched her bleeding fingers from the rock.

The resistance was brief, and in years to come, long after the belligerent Captain Mason had sailed his tall ship up the Pootatuck to calm the noise of the renegade Ansantaway, the granite ledge was pointed out to those who passed through Stratford. For hornblende streaks now etched the granite surface in the image of fingermarks.

The settlers swore these marks had not been there before.